BARBARIAN'S TEASE

A SCIFI ALIEN ROMANCE

RUBY DIXON

RUBY DIXON

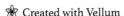 Created with Vellum

BARBARIAN'S TEASE

It should have been a one-night stand.

I never intended to seduce Taushen, but things happened. I don't dwell on the past and while it was great, I'm not looking for a relationship. Of course, try telling that to Taushen. The big blue alien's in love after one night, and it's making things darn awkward. We've got bigger problems than whether or not I'm his woman, like the 'cargo' of the space ship that landed here.

But Taushen's not giving up. He thinks I'm his mate.

And he'll do anything to keep me.

WHAT HAS GONE BEFORE

Aliens are real, and they're aware of Earth. Several human women have been abducted by aliens referred to as "Little Green Men." Some are kept in stasis pods, and some are kept in a pen inside a spaceship, all waiting for sale on an extraterrestrial black market. While the captive humans staged a breakout, the aliens had ship trouble and dumped their living cargo on the nearest inhabitable planet. It is a wintry, desolate place, full of strange wildlife...and stranger people. The humans are not the only species to be abandoned.

The sa-khui, a tribe of massive, horned, blue aliens, thrive on the icy planet. They hunt and forage and live as barbarians, descendants of a long-ago people, who have learned to adapt to the harsh world. The most crucial of adaptions? That of the *khui*, a symbiotic life form that lives inside the host and ensures its well-being. Every creature has a khui, and those without will die within a week, sickened by the air itself. Rescued by the sa-khui, the human women take on a khui symbiont, forever leaving behind any hopes of returning to Earth.

The khui has an unusual side effect on its host: if a compatible pairing is found, the khui will begin to vibrate a song in each host's chest. This is called resonance and is greatly prized by the sa-khui. Only with resonance will the sa-khui be able to propagate their species. The sa-khui, whose numbers were dwindling due to a lack of females in their tribe, were overjoyed when several males begin to resonate to human females, thus ensuring the bonding of both peoples and the life of the newly integrated tribe. A male sa-khui is fiercely devoted to his mate, and one by one, each human woman was claimed by a male hunter. Families have been created, and the tribe is now full of happy families and young kits. As time has passed, more humans females have been found and successfully integrated into the small tribe.

Nearly eight human years have passed since that first band of survivors arrived. Now, directed by a lonely hunter, a spaceship that chanced upon their planet has brought back five new human women. Once slaves, they are adjusting to their new life on the ice planet. Some resonated immediately and cling to their new mates. Others are still settling in.

No one is prepared for the spaceship, the *Tranquil Lady*, to arrive again...or for rogue slavers to appear. The old crew was killed, and many of the sa-khui and their humans are taken captive. It is only through the heroic efforts of a left-behind pair that the slavers are defeated and the others freed once more. Upon exploration of the enemy ship, it is discovered that more slaves—twenty of them, in fact—were waiting to be transported to the black market.

Now the peaceful barbarian tribe must decide what to do with not only a hijacked spaceship, but the dubious cargo inside...

BROOKE

"*B*uh-brukh, are you all right?" Farli gives me a curious look over her shoulder. "You seem angry this day."

I grit my teeth, my hands full of strands of her long, thick hair. Buh-brukh. Again with the Buh-brukh. I don't bother correcting her—as I have many times in the past—that my name isn't "Buh-brukh" but "Brooke." No matter how many times I correct the tribe in a nice, polite voice, they never say my name right. Not that anyone's name is pronounced correctly. Gail is Shail, because no one can say a "G" sound correctly. Summer is something more like Sooh-murrh. And Georgie is Shorshie. I suppose I should be lucky that I only stuttered when someone asked me my name, and so it's Buh-brukh for now and forever in their minds. I could have retorted with, "It's Brooke, asshole," and then I'd be stuck with Brukh-Asshole for the rest of my days.

Doesn't matter. Buh-brukh is what has stuck. Most of the time, I don't mind. It's even cute when it comes out of the mouth of one of the adorable, tiny-horned kits that wander around the tribe.

Of course, there's one tribesmate in particular that has taken great pains to learn my real name. Taushen calls me Brooke...

But Taushen can also jump off a cliff for all I care. I'm done with his ass.

Just thinking about the male sa-khui makes me grit my teeth. It's useless wasting breath—or thoughts—on someone like him. So I shrug, braiding Farli's hair a little tighter. All these sa-khui are so competent and skilled it makes me second-guess myself. I may not be a great huntress like Farli or Liz, and I'm not terrific with electronics like Harlow, but being a hairdresser means I can make a fierce braid and that I can manage to look great even on a remote iceball planet. Since that's the skill set I've got, I use it. Harlow's got a pair of bright red French braids this day, and my own hair is done in a pink fishtail tail over one shoulder. For Farli, I'm doing a starburst coronet of braids—not so easy with someone that has a pair of horns. But her hair's so thick it's going to look downright magnificent when I'm done. Not that it's hard for Farli to look magnificent. All she has to do is stand there, all pretty blue skin and lean, muscular body and proud horns. Someone like me with nothing going for her but boobs and an ability to braid has to play up her assets.

But when Farli tries to turn around and look at me again, it's clear she's wanting an answer as to why I seem "angry." There's a million things that pour through my head as to how I could answer, but all of them sound bitter, and I'm determined not to be that person. "Just thinking," I tell her brightly.

Nothing more than that, no siree.

"Are you...what is the word." Farli pauses for a moment, trying to choose her thoughts carefully. "Like Ell-ee? Your head hurts after what we endured?"

Is she asking if I'm traumatized by what happened? It's sweet of her to worry. We've been through a lot lately, especially us new humans. First we're kidnapped from Earth, and then not much longer after that, we're dragged to the ice planet, given cooties, and told this is our new home forever and ever. Then, bad guys show up, take us all captive again, and come this close to selling us as slaves back on the intergalactic black market. It's a lot to process.

Truth be told, the alien hijack and almost-kidnapping was scary, but it had a good ending. We're still here on the ice planet. It was actually less traumatic than my last experience. No one stripped me naked and prodded me or checked my teeth. No one pinched my flanks or sniffed my hair or groped me. No one stole me away from everything I've ever known.

Except for one particular incident, it actually went much better than expected when one's captured by slavers. "I'm okay," I tell her. I want to ask if she's okay, honestly. I think Earth people are a little more jaded than the sa-khui. We've had television to make us a little more immune to things like murder and slavery and all kinds of heinous shit. To Farli and her people, everyone's happy and huggy and everything turns out well. It's like they're living in some sort of Disney movie.

If anyone's going to be traumatized, it's them. I'm getting better every day about moving past the bad shit. Did I cry a lot in the beginning? Yes. But all my tears are dried up. I guess this is what they mean when they say survival mode kicks in. I think if more aliens landed and attacked, I wouldn't even cry at that point. I'd try to figure out what it takes to stay alive.

In the end, that's all that's important—getting to the next day.

There's a clatter of footsteps up the ramp, and I freeze, waiting to see who pops inside the ship. But it's only Rukh, Harlow's almost-feral mate. I'd smile at him in greeting, but I know he won't smile back. He's been in a real mood ever since shit went down—not that I blame him. Both he and Harlow are missing their little son something fierce. I just nod at him in acknowledgment and then go back to braiding Farli's hair as she twitches in her seat. For all that she's graceful and strong, she's a squirmy sort.

And I forgot to answer her again. Oops. Am I traumatized? "I'm not going to go all Elly and not bathe for months if that's what you're asking." Elly has every right to be how she is. She's had a really rough life, and I don't hold it against her...but at the same time, I like clean hair far too much to ever go that far.

Farli chuckles, folding her legs under her and moving again, disturbing my careful braiding. "I was merely curious. You have been less...friendly with Taushen. I wondered if he said something cruel."

Oh, did she notice the chill between us? I guess we've been a little obvious in our mutual disdain for one another ever since...the Incident. Not that I want to think about—or talk about—said incident. I grab another section of her thick hair and weave it into her dark braid, continuing my circle around the crown of her head. What to say about Taushen that won't be considered rude and will end the discussion? Hmm. "It wasn't anything he *said*," I edge after a few.

It was definitely something he *did*, though. The dick.

The answer seems to satisfy Farli, and she remains quiet and still while I braid yet another section into her crown. I'm pleased with how it's turning out, and just the sight of my handiwork relaxes the knot in my stomach that's been present ever since the Incident.

A stiff breeze blows in, ruffling my own unbraided hair and carrying with it the sound of Chompy's bleating. Farli chuckles, a happy little sigh escaping her.

She's so easy to please. I'm envious.

We're seated just inside the Tranquil Lady, at the top of the ramp that leads to the outside. Farli's pet llama-thing is pawing at the snow below and nipping at frozen roots underneath. She wants him to stay close, but since he was pooping all over the deck, we decided to set up here so I could do her hair. It's a good spot, with a fresh breeze...and an easy exit in case we have to run. Which might be silly to think about, given that the last enemies had laser guns, but I still consider such things.

After being held captive twice now, you start to keep an eye on every escape route in the nearby area. Just in case.

Of course, sitting at the entrance of the ramp means that we're in a high traffic area. The hunters have to come through here to get to the interior of the ship, and we're staying in the Tranquil Lady until we figure out what to do with her. She's in better working order than the ancient ship, and she's got guns. Plus, Mardok has working knowledge of how to run everything on this ship.

And then there's the cargo, of course. Until it's decided what to do with it—them, I guess—we're staying here to keep an eye on things.

Not my favorite choice, but the room I'm staying in has running water, a toilet, and oh, no Taushen, so it's a win.

As if our thoughts have summoned him, Taushen enters the spaceship hold next, coming up the ramp. Of course it's Taushen, because I have the worst luck imaginable and naturally I'd run into him when I'd rather never see him again.

I watch him out of the corner of my eye as he saunters up the ramp. He's got a spear in hand, a hopper corpse in the other. An alien guy shouldn't look that good, I decide. A swish of a tail shouldn't be sexy. Horns shouldn't make me get all faint at the way they arch and curl around his head. Blue skin and bulging muscles shouldn't do a thing for me. A fur loincloth should be stupid.

Stupid, I tell you.

Especially since I know how much he's packing under that little scrap of leather. It's doubly stupid, then. He needs more fabric.

And I should tell him that, but it'd mean I'd have to talk to him, and I've vowed not to do that anymore. So I just give a haughty sniff and pretend to concentrate really, really hard on Farli's hair.

Taushen pauses at the top of the ramp at the sight of us. He nods at Farli and gives me a cold look. "Buh-brukh," he murmurs, then saunters past.

Oh, *burn*. That ass. I know very well that he knows how to say my name correctly. He said it just fucking fine when he was balls deep inside me.

But I suppose that's my fault, too, since I'm the one that seduced him.

Farli hisses, pulling away from my hands. "You are making my mane a very tight cord today."

Oops. Did I pull too hard? "Sorry. I'll pay more attention." Especially considering that Taushen's still lingering nearby. I don't want him to hear that. I don't want him to think that I'm even dwelling on him for one hot second. I pat Farli's shoulder and try to forget all about Taushen, and that night in the ship. It didn't mean anything, just like I told him then.

No idea why he's continuing to be a huge dick about it. I'm pretty sure these people are familiar with the concept of "one and done." And I'm also pretty sure that the situation we were in was an obvious one that meant no strings attached. And the sex was good. Really good.

But for some reason, Taushen's had a burr up his butt ever since.

And if he's expecting me to go to him and apologize for seducing him to save both of our lives? He's going to be waiting a long, long damn time.

Because I am not that girl. And I can hold a grudge for-mother-fucking-ever.

Then, Taushen leaves. He doesn't say anything else, just up and leaves. I don't care. I tell myself I couldn't give a rat's ass if he walked right into the engine room and turned into a crisp. It'd serve him right.

I'm a bad liar, even to myself, though. I chew on the inside of my cheek as I finish braiding Farli's crown and use a small bit of leather to tie the end off. If I had bobby pins, I'd pin the tail end into her braid and hide it so it looks like a perfect circle. I don't have that, though, so I just do a bit of artful tucking into the loops and hide it as best I can. "There. You're more beautiful than ever now."

She touches her braid, a smile brightening her face. "Shall I go show Mardok?"

"Only if you want him to throw you down and ravish you like the glorious creature you are," I tease, my spirits a little lighter at her happiness.

"That is exactly what I wish to happen," she exclaims, her expression eager. Then, she sighs. "But I should not distract him from his work."

"I should see what Harlow needs me to do," I tell her. I get to my feet, dusting off my leather tunic of any stray strands of Farli's hair. "After all, I stayed behind to help her, right? Might as well do it."

"Might as well," Farli echoes, agreeing. An impish look crosses her face. "I am still going to find Mardok and show him my mane, though."

"You do that," I say, chuckling. At least someone's determined to have a good day. That's the thing with Farli—nothing gets her down. She's sunshine personified, and I have to admire that.

The rest of us are having a harder time keeping that cheer going. Especially Harlow. When I make it to the far end of the ship in the med bay, where she's working, her eyes are suspiciously red as she makes notes on her electronic pad-thingy. It's kind of like an iPad from back on Earth, except it responds to hand flicks instead of tapping, and so when she uses it, it looks a bit like her hand is spasming. She told me the other day that it also responds to pupil movements, but it doesn't read our eyes correctly, thanks to the glow from the khui within. So, hand-twitches it is. Rukh hovers in a corner of the room, spear in his grip, looking like a really big blue vulture. I know he hates to leave Harlow alone. Can't blame him. Not after what we recently went through. "Hey, Harlow," I say, keeping my voice cheerful to try and bring her up, too. Seems kind of insipid to ask her how she's doing this morning, so I opt for humor instead. "You look like you've lost weight."

Harlow's eyes widen and she chuckles, patting her heavily pregnant belly. "I do, huh?"

"Oh yeah, at least a pound," I say cheerily. "So, what can I help with today?"

She looks at the scatter of broken components spread out on a table, a helpless look on her face. Some of them are larger—one even looks like a hair dryer—and some are so small that they're no bigger than my pinky nail. Given that there's literally a hundred of them neatly spread out before her, it looks like the world's crappiest jigsaw puzzle. "Let me think. Not this—it'd take more time to explain this than it would for me to just do it myself."

"Darn." Secretly, I'm glad. I'm not good with puzzles.

Her expression brightens. "You can go check on the pods. It's about time for the morning rounds anyhow." She turns and moves to Rukh's side, caressing his shoulder as she picks up another tablet on the table near him. I don't miss the way he softens when she approaches, or the way he strokes her fingers lightly as she touches him. There's so much fierce love for her in his eyes that it hurts me to look at it.

Well, that and it makes me envious, too. I'd love for someone to give me a look as hot as that one, especially years into a relationship.

Harlow turns away from him and waddles toward me, holding out the pad. "You remember how to operate this?"

"No? Wait." I make a jerk-off motion in front of the pad. "Huh, didn't turn it on."

Harlow snort-giggles. "Very funny." She does a double finger wiggle in the corner, and the screen changes. "Here are the notes. You remember—"

"I do, yup," I tell her before she can launch into the explanation. I immediately feel bad for cutting her off and give her a smile. "Sorry. It's just not my favorite chore."

"Oh." She bites her lip. "Well...maybe I can think of something else."

"It's okay," I tell her as Rukh starts to glare in my direction. I know what he's thinking—don't stress out the already-stressed pregnant lady. I don't want to, either. I just need to suck it up. "It's something I can do, and I'm glad to help. I guess I'll head out."

"Thank you, Brooke. It really is appreciated."

"Just send someone after me if I don't come back in an hour," I joke. Sorta.

Except I'm not joking all that much, I think, as I head out of the med bay and down one of the dark, twisting metal halls of The Tranquil Lady. The cargo bay creeps me out. It's like something out of a horror movie. But Harlow can't do everything herself, and I did stay behind to help. And I'm an adult. I shouldn't be scared of people sleeping in coffin-like things. They're harmless. They're asleep. They won't even know I'm there.

The more I tell myself that, maybe I'll start to believe it.

For all that the ship looks massive outside, on the inside it's a lot smaller. There are a lot of passageways, but the actual rooms themselves aren't very big, except for the cargo bay. It's clear that's where most of the room is allocated, and going from the normal-sized tunnels to the big, yawning cargo bay is always a bit eerie. Add in the fact that it's atmospherically dark, and it's really not helping my horror movie ideas.

"You stayed behind to help, you ninny," I tell myself, the closest thing I can get to a self-pep-talk. "So quit your bitching."

Since we discovered the twenty pods of unconscious people that the slavers had with them, one of the focuses of our group—in addition to dismantling or removing any signals, traces, or records of our planet that might be stored—is keeping them safe.

Safe, and still securely in storage, asleep.

The consensus is that they're slaves, after all. Slaves being carted off by slavers to take to the black market. Just what kind of slaves, though, we don't know. There are four men, and they all look fierce and terrifying. Of course, I thought the sa-khui were fearsome when I first saw them, too, and now I'm no longer scared of them. The other sixteen are human women. All of them pose a problem. They could be innocent women dragged from their beds in the middle of the night—like me—or they could be humans who have been in the "system" so long that they've half forgotten how to be human, like Elly. And the guys? None of them are human, so no one knows anything about them. For now, it's kinder to leave them asleep, where they don't know what's going on, until the sa-khui chief, Vektal, arrives.

He's going to decide if we wake them up, and what we do with the ship.

I move down the long row of pods in the cargo bay, thinking about the people sleeping here. Was I in one of these when I was kidnapped? If so, how long was I under? I don't remember anything like this. I just remember going to sleep after a party and waking up and finding myself in a holding cell, surrounded by aliens. I had no clothes, and for a while, I thought it was just a really vivid bad dream. After a few days, when I didn't wake up, I had to accept the fact that it was reality, and a waking nightmare. I shudder, thinking of the aliens that poked and prodded me, exclaiming over my hair and my boobs. Oddly enough, I thought my large boobs were going to paint a target on me, like they did back when I was in middle school and grew into double-D-cups long before the other girls filled out A-cups. Turns out that aliens aren't much fans of big boobs, and I got rejected by more weird-looking alien buyers than the small-breasted girls.

God bless my great big tatas.

I move to the first of the coffins—excuse me, pods—and tap the button on the top corner of the control panel. A bright flood of weird-looking characters covers the small screen, looking like nothing more than a bunch of dashes, wiggles, and dots. Space cuneiform, I decide, comparing the message to the one written on my tablet. I can't read alien writing, but Harlow has walked me through enough to show me what the screen should look like when I punch the button, and so I compare the characters, wiggle by painstaking squiggle, to make sure that everything matches up. If something doesn't, I have to go get Harlow or Mardok because there's a problem of some kind.

As jobs go, this is a pretty easy one. Time consuming, but easy. I compare writing, check each pod, and go. But because I'm a chicken, it creeps me out. It's so quiet in the cargo bay, and the room's so big. And I'm so alone with a bunch of "dead"-seeming people. Maybe that's why it freaks me out. Or maybe it's their expressions, I decide as I lean over the pod to stare into the sleeping face of one of the strangers. They look dead, or like mannequins. No breath fogs the glass on the pod, and they don't twitch or move like people do in sleep. They're completely and utterly still, like dolls waiting to be taken out of the box to be played with. The analogy creeps me out, because it's far too real. I gaze down at the face of the guy in the pod, wondering about him. He's a strange shimmering gold all over, with a pattern on his skin that looks almost like scales, and his hair is thick and sticks up like an animal mane—

"Buh-brukh," a voice says, and I yelp, jerking backward in surprise.

I nearly drop the tablet in my hands, scrambling to hold on to it. "Jesus, you scared the shit out of me, Taushen. Don't fucking *do* that!"

"Do what?" He leans to one side in the doorway, the picture of insolence. His expression is hard. "Address you by name?"

"Sneak up on me," I snap at him. "I realize you blue dudes have catlike stealth, but I'm a human and I can't hear when you *sneak* up." I clutch the tablet hard and move on to coffin number two. "And don't think I didn't notice that little jab about my name, dickface."

He snorts. "I came to ask if you needed assistance with anything."

"If I want your help, I'll tell you," I say, giving him my sweetest, fakest smile, and lean over the second coffin and jab the button. Wiggles flood the screen, but I'm not going to be able to compare the two until Taushen leaves and stops distracting me. I stare at the screen anyhow, doing my best to look busy.

"Like that night we were trapped together?"

I jerk upright, gasping at him. "How dare you! I saved our lives."

His jaw flexes and he looks pissed. "Perhaps I did not wish to be saved."

"Really? I didn't notice you protesting when I touched you. Or when you grabbed my tits and pushed my thighs apart. Or when you groaned my name as you came. *Twice.*" I give him a tight smile. "During which of those times did you protest? Can you refresh my memory? I must not be remembering correctly."

Taushen's eyes narrow and he straightens. For a moment, he looks like he wants to say something—and it's not something nice. Instead, though, he just whirls on one foot and storms away in a cloud of black hair.

"Fuck you, too," I mutter, and try to get back to work.

Of course, I can't. I'm trembling as I think about that night.

Everything changed that night, and I don't know if I'm ever going to forget how it felt.

2

BROOKE

One Week Ago

"*A* ship's landing," Gail calls out, surprised. "Come and see."

I rouse myself from my furs, but just a little. I'm supposed to be sick, after all. Summer would kill me if she knew that I'd bailed out on our fruit-gathering run just because I wanted to avoid a man.

One man in particular.

Taushen.

I don't know what to make of that particular sa-khui male. The married—sorry, *mated*—ones are all very nice and super devoted to their wives. The single ones are a lot harder to make heads or tails of. I've tried flirting—and flirting heavily—to test the waters. Being a pretty girl can be powerful. Considering I've got no skills except hairdressing, I'm at a distinct disadvantage here in the wild. If the only things I've got going for me are a vagina and boobs, I'm going to have to use them to the best of my ability. It doesn't work out so well, though. Of the single men, Harrec is clearly enamored of Kate, and Warrek might as well be a statue. Only Taushen replies to my flirting, and it's usually with a scowl. It's clear that he doesn't find me attractive and doesn't like me in the slightest.

So when I heard that Warrek, Summer, me, and Taushen were all supposed to go to the fruit caves overnight to gather supplies? I feigned cramps...and then a migraine, just to cover my bases. No way am I going on that trip. Maybe that makes me a jerk, but the thought of Taushen glaring at me all day when I try to be friendly just makes me shrivel up inside a little.

"I'm serious," Gail says, standing in the doorway of the Elders' Ship and gazing out into the snowy sky. "It's a ship. I know you feel lousy right now, but come look and tell me I'm not crazy."

She's not going to let this go until I come and check it out. With a groan, I drag myself out of bed and stagger over to where she's standing. "What? Are you sure it's not just a big bird?" I peer past her shoulder and then pause in surprise. Huh. It *is* a ship. "Doesn't that look like..."

"The ship we got here on? Yup. Unless all alien ships look the same." Gail looks worried.

"Doesn't look like this one," I point out. It's all sleek-looking, whereas the one we're on is more blobby and rounded. Of course, that might be the heaps of snow covering it or the fact that it's falling down around our ears.

"No, you're right." She presses her fingers to her mouth and then glances over at me. "You don't think they're coming back to get us, do you?"

I clutch at her arm, sick at the thought. The people that brought us here bought us as slaves and then dumped us as a "favor" to the tribe here. While I'm grateful I'm not a slave anymore, I'd also rather be back on Earth. But there's no reason for them to come back...unless it's what Gail's saying. They're coming back to grab us. "Should we hide?"

"Is that one of the flying caves?" a voice booms out. It's Vaza, Gail's blue boyfriend. He's older than the others, though you wouldn't know it based off of how he looks. Other than a few gray streaks in his black hair, he's just as built as all these other guys. "Shail, did you see?"

"I saw," she tells him. "Vaza, what if they're here to take us back?" She puts an arm around my shoulders, and I'm not sure if it's because she thinks I need the support, or if she needs someone to hang on to.

"Never," he says staunchly. "You are here now. You have a khui. It cannot be stolen from you."

Vaza may be sure about that, but I seem to recall a lot of medical technology on the ship, and I'm not sure he's right. Either way, it doesn't ease my fears.

Nor Gail's, it seems. She still casts worried looks at the doorway. "Should we go out and say hello?"

We watch as the ship settles onto the snow close by. The ramp lowers, but no one gets out. The hairs on the back of my neck prickle.

"Did you hear something?" Harrec pushes his way into the main living area of the ship, a fur blanket wrapped around his hips. He's naked otherwise, and behind him, a disheveled Kate follows, almost as nude. Clearly the ship landing interrupted some hanky-panky.

Rukh and Harlow appear out of another passageway, Rukhar holding his mother's hand. Behind them are Farli and Mardok, and in the space of a breath, Bek and Elly appear as well. Well, crap. Everyone's here now except Taushen, Warrek, and Summer, who are off at the fruit cave. At least Taushen's not here to bug me.

"What was that?" someone asks.

"They have returned," says a voice behind me. Oh no. I look at the ramp into the Elders' Ship to see Taushen coming inside. He looks slightly sweaty, as if he ran all the way here.

Vaza exclaims at the sight of him. "Taushen? Why have you returned?"

"It is not important." He flicks a quick look at me and then focuses on the others. "Suh-mer and Warrek continued on to the fruit caves. I did not, and came back just in time to see the new cave land."

"It's a ship," I correct him crabbily. "It's not a flying cave. It's a spaceship."

"It's fine," Gail says in a soothing voice, patting my shoulder. She casts another worried look at Vaza. "But shouldn't we go out and say hello?"

"Of course," Vaza booms, ever-cheerful. He gives Gail another adoring look. "Anything for you."

"Not just for her," I mutter, crossing my arms, but Gail nudges me.

"I will go with you," Harrec says, knotting the fur at his waist and moving to Vaza's side. Rukh surges forward, too.

Bek touches Elly's cheek. "Stay here, safe with the other females. I will find out what is happening."

She nods, and I can see she's trembling, her shoulders hunched. Poor Elly. I have a sick knot in my gut at the thought of the Tranquil Lady returning, because I don't want to be taken back. I can't imagine the hell that she's going through right now, given that she was a slave for a lot longer than the rest of us.

Gail must sense how Elly's feeling, because she immediately crosses over to her side and grabs one of the furs from my bed, wrapping it around Elly. "Come sit down, honey. You're pale." She pulls Elly toward the fire, clucking over her.

"No, no," I mutter to myself. "I'm fine now, Gail. Really. I didn't need that blanket."

Taushen snorts, the only person close enough to hear my grumblings.

I shoot him a quick look, hoping he doesn't expose my crankiness to the others, but he says nothing. He's watching the other hunters head down the ramp, led by Vaza with Mardok not far behind him. "Shouldn't you go join them?" I ask him, hoping he'll leave.

But he only shakes his head and grips his spear tightly in one hand, gaze on the snowy plain that the others are crossing. "Someone must guard the females."

I'm about to point out that we shouldn't need guarding from the crew of the Tranquil Lady when Vaza stumbles and falls down. It's so unlike one of the graceful sa-khui that I gasp in surprise. But when Taushen flings himself in front of me, a growl in his throat, I realize Vaza didn't fall down by accident after all.

He's been shot.

"What's happening?" I whisper, trying to peer over Taushen's shoulder. He's well over a foot taller than me, and I can't see, so I grab his brawny blue bicep and try to peek around him.

Taushen growls low in his throat, and for a moment I think he's mad at me for trying to get around him—but then I see a bright flash. There's a man standing on the ramp of the other ship, a long, thin weapon propped at his shoulder just like a rifle. At least, I think it's a man. It's two-legged, but he's got an orange bubblehead and round, fishlike eyes. He stands over Vaza's fallen body and nudges it with the end of his gun. I realize with horror that Vaza's not the only one on the ground, and there are others scattered in the snow. As I watch, another orange alien comes down the ramp, too. He's got a gun as well and waves it at the wreck of the ship we're currently standing in.

Someone moans behind me. It's Gail. "Are they dead?" she whispers.

"They are twitching," Taushen says, voice cold. His grip is tight on the door jamb. "But they do not move otherwise."

"Maybe...maybe they shocked them?" I ask. I can't look away. The sa-khui are scattered in the snow before the newcomers, and it's clear they tried to race away the moment they started shooting. "I didn't hear gunshots, but maybe they're not regular guns..."

"Harrec," Kate sobs, clutching at the doorframe. "We have to do something." Behind her, Harlow is pale, clutching her son close.

I look to Taushen, but he's clearly torn. He shifts in place, as if he wants to lunge after the others, but he keeps glancing back at the human women clustered in the doorway, and I can practically read his mind. He wants to spring to the defense of the others... but he also doesn't want to abandon us since he's established himself as our protector.

One of the aliens looks up at our ship and nods. He sees us standing there and calls something out in a strange tongue. I can't make out what he's saying, but I can guess it. Come out if you want to live. The muzzle of his gun is lowered ever so slightly, as if to reassure us.

"Should we go out?" I whisper. Elly shrinks down, curling into a ball on the floor. Her eyes are huge and staring out at the snow, as if silently willing Bek to get up. I'm sick at the heartbreak in her eyes. Sick at all of this. Is there no safe place in the universe?

"What did they say?" Farli asks.

"Nothing good," Taushen says grimly. "Stay here, all of you."

He strides forward a footstep, then pauses and shoves his spear into my hand. "Guard them."

Wide-eyed, I nod. The thought of going up against men with guns with a bone spear is terrifying, but what choice do I have? My heart is hammering in my chest, and I'm so freaking scared I feel like I can't breathe.

Taushen turns back around to the strange aliens and takes a few slow steps forward. He's not more than halfway down the short ramp when the alien lifts his gun, pointing it at Taushen, and barks a new order. Taushen pauses.

"I think they want us to go with him," I whisper to the others.

Gail nods and puts an arm around a trembling, sheet-white Elly. Kate's sobbing, but she moves next to me, and Farli moves to my other side. I look for Harlow, but she's receded into the shadows. I can't blame her—she's got a kid on her arm and one in her belly to think about.

"Stay behind me," Taushen warns us. "Do not make any sudden moves. Let me protect you."

Brave words, but as the cluster of us moves slowly forward, I don't think there's anything he can do. There's nothing any of us can do except surrender.

3

BROOKE

$\mathcal{T}$hings seem to happen in a cascade after that. We're all dragged forward and forced to drop to our knees in the snow, kneeling in front of the enemy while they discuss things in their strange, barking language. Harlow's dragged out of the ship a short time later and sobs loudly at the sight of her mate fallen in the snow. The aliens let her keep Rukhar with her, and they seem fascinated by her big belly, murmuring to each other about it while we wait. Taushen is dragged on board the ship, unwilling but also not fighting. He just gazes at us with bitter frustration in his eyes, and it's clear to me he wants to do something to stop this, but he knows trying anything would just result in his going down like the rest of the men.

We sit in the snow and watch as one by one, the unconscious men are dragged into the ship. There are at least four orange aliens and no sign of the old crew of the Tranquil Lady, and the gnawing worry in my stomach won't go away.

This is bad. This is really, really bad.

At some point, Harrec regains consciousness and tries to tackle one of our alien captors, which ends up in him just getting shocked unconscious again. Kate breaks into fits of tears, and the tears keep flowing when they bring out her tiny kitten and take him, too. Farli is silent as her pet, Chompy, is roped and dragged on board the ship. Her hand is on her belly, and she watches with fierce, narrowed eyes as the remaining sa-khui men are collared as they are unconscious.

I remember those collars. Shock collars.

Slave collars.

We're going to be sold into slavery all over again.

The realization makes me want to throw up. I can tell Elly and Gail realize the same thing—there's a dead look in their eyes as we watch the unconscious men get collared and taken away. Back to the hell we just got rescued from.

It seems so very unfair. Life can't play this cruel a joke on us, can it?

One of the aliens comes toward us, waving his gun. He says something and it sounds like nothing more than crackling coming from his throat. I can't make heads or tails of it.

When no one speaks up to answer him, I glance around. Kate's still crying, and Farli is glaring silently. Both Elly and Gail look traumatized. They were both slaves for a lot longer than I was, and I understand. I think of how hard I cried when I first arrived here. Eventually I got used to things. I grew stronger. I can survive this, too. So I swallow hard and look at the waiting alien. "We can't understand you. We speak English."

He cocks his head, and those fish-eyes focus on me. "Hain-glish?" he says after a moment. "Yuuurth Hainglish?"

"That's the one," I say dully. "Yurth Hainglish."

"Youuu haf breeeding ffeemalesss," he comments, nudging his gun at Harlow. She gets to her feet, tears streaking her freckled face. "Preknannnt?"

She nods, sniffling.

I'm surprised that they're gentle when they put the shock collar around her slender throat, and they don't even bother with putting one on Rukhar. He's too little, I suspect, and we all know he's not going anywhere. He clings to his mother's hand as they lead her into the ship.

The orange alien turns to me. "Whhhisssh one is hurrr mayyyl?"

He wants to know who she's married to? I hesitate, because I'm not sure if I should give up that kind of information. Then again, what does it hurt? We're already captured. They shouldn't care unless they want to keep them together. "His name is Rukh. I can show you which one he is if you bring me to them."

The other women stare at me, aghast, like I just agreed to blow our alien captors. Can't they see what I'm doing? Maybe not. I'll have to explain later. For now, it's important that I keep a family together if I can.

When the other alien comes back out with a slave collar, they confer with more of their strange, crackling language and point at me. I hug my arms to my chest, shivering and hoping I didn't screw things up for Harlow and Rukh. The new alien comes to my side and puts the collar on me while I stand meekly still, even if the urge to run is screaming through my head. At least Summer and Warrek didn't get captured. God, I should have gone to the fruit cave with them and I wouldn't be here right now. Stupid

Taushen should have stayed with them. Now he's as screwed as we are.

The orange alien points into the ship. "Innnnsssssside."

I head up the ramp, even though it feels like every step is taking me away from my freedom. There's a huge knot in my throat, but I choke it back. Or try to. I mostly just sound like I'm gurgling miserably.

The alien leads me down a hall in the ship, and I swallow hard at the sight of dark blood spattered on the metallic walls. There are old, dried stains on the flooring that tell me that this probably wasn't a peaceful takeover of the ship. I don't know how they found us, but I wonder if the old crew sold us out. But I think of Mardok, who was taken captive with the rest of the men. Maybe not. Maybe things are just as awful as they seem. The alien at my side shoulders his weapon and punches buttons on the wall panel, and the door slides into the wall with a hiss. Inside, there's an unconscious sa-khui male—Harrec.

"Hrrr mayyyl?" the alien asks me. "They are pair?"

"Not this one," I tell him, and then an idea occurs to me. If they're keeping one couple together... "This one is the male of the very tall white-haired female. She is pregnant with his child."

He frowns. "They are pair?" he repeats again.

"A mating pair, yes. Very compatible." What else do slavers look for in mating pairs? "They will breed many strong babies." So they can all grow up as slaves? Ugh, I'm grossing myself out with even suggesting such a thing, but I also know Kate's terrified for Harrec. If I were in her position, I'd want to be with my man. So... if I can influence things, I'm going to try.

I mean, hell, it can't get much worse than this.

The alien stares at me and then taps something out on his armband. A moment later, a new alien appears, this one without a gun but in a sleek dark bodysuit that emphasizes their weird anatomy. His ribcage looks truncated and his hipbones jut out like a tinkertoy alien that was put together weirdly. He barks something at the other in their strange language.

My companion speaks, gesturing at me, then at the room Harrec's locked into. They both look at me. "Feeeemayyyyl is wif younnnng?"

I nod. "The one with the white hair. Run a pregnancy test on her if you don't believe me."

They exchange a look. "Wait heeeere," the second alien says, and gets out something that looks like an iPad. He returns a few short minutes later and nods at his friend. "She carries."

"Breeding pairrr," the other says. "More moneyyyy."

"There are several breeding pairs," I point out. "Lots and lots of money. I can show you which ones."

The second alien looks at me with those weird, unblinking eyes. "You...brreeeding pairrrr?"

"Me? No. No mate."

They look at me, and then one grabs my hand, pinching the skin on the back of it. He holds his pad close to my skin. A tiny needle shoots out and scrapes along my skin, leaving a welt. The alien pauses and studies his pad, then nods. "No mmaaaayyyyt."

The second alien speaks up. "But otherrrrs...breeding pairrrs..."

"Yes, and I can show you all of them."

"Shhhowww," he gargles at me.

So I do. I point out which human belongs with which sa-khui

male. I want to keep the families together, and I hope desperately that they'll see this as a good thing. Even if we get taken away from this planet and the tribe, if I can keep the girls with their men—and Rukhar with his parents—I'll have done something right. The aliens make notes and talk privately to themselves as I give them details. I hope that means they're taking this to heart and I'm not making a mistake. That I'm not selling out my friends. I even tell them that Gail and Vaza are a mated couple, even though Gail swears up and down that she's too old to have kids. I know she'd want to stay with him. I tense up, wondering if the aliens are going to go out and test Gail's blood too, but they only take notes and move on to the next alien.

At the end, we get to Taushen's cell. He's not unconscious, but he's bound hand and foot, facing the opposite wall. All I can see is his broad back and the long hair that sweeps down his shoulders, and his endlessly flicking tail.

"This one isn't mated," I tell them in a low voice, hating that I have to admit the truth. But I can't save Taushen. There's no one else to "hook" him up with even as a lie, and they know he's not mine. We're going to be condemned to the same fate, him and I— sold without a partner and no one else to lean on. I'm not a big fan of Taushen, other than he's easy to look at, but I hate that he's getting the shortest end of the short end of the stick when it comes to this.

Well, him and me both, but I chose my fate, in a way. I chose to pair up the others in the eyes of the enemy, for good or for evil. I'm just hoping it'll work out in their favor.

But the aliens only stare at me and then point at Taushen again. "Maaaayl has no maaaayyyyyt?"

"No mate," I say patiently. Our voices are low, and when the door shuts, I'm glad, because I don't want Taushen to hear me talking with them.

"Femaaayl has no maaaayyt?" The alien points at me with one fat, lobster claw-like finger.

Rut-roh, raggy. This is taking an alarming turn. "Um, no."

The aliens talk in their weird language again, and then one makes a weird wheezing noise. It isn't until he slaps his knobby knee that I realize that was the orange bulb-headed alien version of laughing. Yeesh. I try to wait calmly, even though I'm wanting to tug on the collar on my neck something desperate. Every time I swallow, I can feel it against my throat, and it's making me feel claustrophobic.

Then, one alien leaves. The conversation ends and then just one orange-headed alien remains. It doesn't make me feel any easier, though; he's giving me a look I can only describe as sly, despite his fishy eyes. He gazes at my boobs a little too hard, and I wish I hadn't taken my leather tunic in with a few creative nips under the arms to show off my girls. I want to put my arms over my chest, but that might be too obvious, so I pretend to be blissfully unaware of the situation. Meanwhile, the hairs on the back of my neck are prickling and I can feel a cold sweat coming on.

What am I going to do if they decide that because I'm no pregnant... it's open season on my vagina? What if they rape me? A full-body shudder moves through me, and I fight the urge to vomit, thinking of the lobster-claw fingers again. If they try to touch me, I'll fight. And then what? Get shocked into unconsciousness and sleep through whatever they do? God, I don't know if that's better or worse.

I'm about to whimper aloud, but then the second alien returns again, this time with a small metallic thing. When he unscrews the top and sniffs it, it reminds me suspiciously of a flask. Alcohol? Alien alcohol?

He holds it out to me and indicates that I should drink it.

I swallow hard, gingerly taking the flask. A bit of liquid is in it, no more than a few spoonfuls. "What is this?"

"Drrrink," the alien tells me. As if I didn't know.

I stare at them uneasily. If I refuse, are they going to pour it down my throat anyhow? Maybe I'm too much of a coward to put up a fight, but getting all bruised up isn't going to help things. "Bottoms up," I whisper to myself, and then swig the drink. *Please don't be poison.*

I'm half expecting the drink to burn or taste like vomit. Instead, it's cool going down my throat and tastes a bit like mouthwash. I wrinkle my nose and then hold the flask back out to them. "Done."

The two aliens make that weird wheezing laugh again. God. More laughter? I wonder what I just drank. Alien pee? Are these the frat boys of the space slavers? I try to remain calm and not freak the fuck out, and instead mentally chart any symptoms. I don't feel burning on my tongue or swelling in my throat like I've heard happens with a toxin. I don't feel sweaty anymore. I do feel warm and flushed.

Erm...I feel warm and flushed in *specific* places.

And it's getting worse by the moment.

"Oh god," I whisper. I think I've been roofied with the alien version of Spanish fly. I hug my arms over my breasts tightly. "What did you guys give me?"

One moves to the door of Taushen's cell. He taps calmly on the pad and then, when the door swishes into the wall once more, gestures that I should enter. "Yoooou haf no maaaayl," it croaks at me. "Now we maaaayk maaaaayyyyted paaaair. Maaaaake younnnng. Brrring moooore moneyyyy."

Oh, fuck me.

I hesitate, and when I don't rush gleefully into the cell with Taushen, the second alien shoves me from behind. With a squeak, I pitch forward and stumble into the cell. Whatever was in the drink is making my head swim, and the floor seems to bob and weave a little. I flop to the ground and land on my belly, moaning. God, my tits hurt like I've got my period.

God, my *vagina* hurts. That's...new. It aches and feels empty and throbs with need.

"Well, this fucking sucks," I breathe, rolling onto my back and grabbing my boobs to try to stop the ache. I squeeze open one eye and look over. Taushen is staring down at me, an expression of surprise on his hard face.

"Brooke," he whispers, giving a puzzled look to my tit grab. "What do you do here?"

4

TAUSHEN

*C*aptured.

Shame and anger boil in my belly. Shame that I could not protect the females. Anger that we have been so easily overtaken. Helpless rage joins in. How could I let our people be taken? Why did I not fight to the death?

The answer is as obvious as it is annoying. Brooke and the others needed protecting. They have no one to look after them if I let myself get taken with the others, so I chose to stay behind. Not that it mattered in the end, because I am yet captured. However, capture is not defeat. As long as I am alive, I will fight to free myself and the others. Even now, with my hands bound behind my back by strange rope, I twist ever so slightly in my bonds, waiting for them to loosen.

I have not given up. I will never give up.

The door opens to the cave I am being held inside. It takes all of my willpower not to stiffen or alert them in any way that I have heard. I remain calm and still. I do not twist my hands. Only my tail lashes back and forth, but I cannot stop that no more than I can stop my breathing. I hear the soft sound of Brooke's voice, and it calls up even more intense feelings. I am angry and frustrated that she has been captured, but not surprised.

Brooke. She and the one called Suh-mer are the last unmated females. They are my only chances at a family and kits, and yet again, my khui chooses to remain silent.

I hate it. I hate that it will not choose. I hate that time after time, I have been ignored and that the khuis of others have sung. The initial group of females arrived, and I thought I would surely have a mate amongst them. One by one, though, they resonated to others. Then Li-lah and her sister. Then the five enslaved humans. It is a bountiful feast for the sa-khui amongst the prized and once-rare females. My friends and hunter companions have paired up, mated, started families...

And yet I remain alone.

My khui is either flawed or too choosy. No, I realize bitterly. It is not the khui that is flawed, it is me. A khui always selects the best mate to make kits with a female. The fact that I have not been chosen tells me that there is something wrong with me that makes me a poor mate to any female. It is a thought that has eaten at me for turns.

The one thing I want the most, I will never get, and I do not even get an explanation as to why.

I hear Brooke's voice again as she speaks with someone. Her voice is too low, her conversation happening too far away for me to hear. Thinking about her fills me with lust...and scorn. When she first arrived here, she gave me interested looks and flirted, letting me know she found me attractive. Her attentions filled me with such hope. Perhaps if I did not resonate, I would at least have a pleasure-mate to spend my time with. Someone to ease the loneliness. It soon became clear to me that Brooke flirted with all the males to get what she wanted. I was not special in her eyes. When she gave me sweet looks, it was because she wanted her pack carried or she wanted someone to give her an extra fur for her bed. It was not because she wanted my attention. She just wanted me to give her things or do things for her.

My interest in her soured after that, even if I cannot deny that she is an attractive female. Like most humans, she has enlarged teats, but Brooke's are bigger than most, and they jiggle in the most enticing of ways when she walks. I try not to notice...but I notice. Just like I notice that her mane is a strange color, like the edges of the dawn against the mountains...but it is growing in a dark, rich brown against her scalp. I notice she does not have a tail. I notice that she makes happy little noises in her sleep. I notice that she has long lashes and that she has two laughs—her pretend laugh she uses to get males to do things for her, and a smaller, almost shy chuckle that seems more sincere.

I should not notice these things about a human I have distaste for, but I do.

So that leaves Suh-mer...but she has not held my interest. She is kind, but she does not have the shy chuckle that makes my sac tighten.

So, alone I remain.

But then the doors to my cave shut, and a figure stumbles and lands on the ground nearby. I look over to see Brooke, her colorful mane tumbled about her face.

She moans and cups her teats, shuddering on the floor.

The doors shut behind us, and then we are alone. Brooke has

been left with me. Strange. I glance around, wondering if this is a trap. When no one emerges, I lean closer to her. "Brooke? What do you do here?"

She sits up slowly. She blinks, a little unfocused, her eyes seemingly huge in her delicate human face. "Taushen," she murmurs, her gaze fixed on me at last. There's a breathless quality to her tone that is surprising. "Are you...okay?"

I glance at the door before twisting my hands in my bonds again. "Well enough. How are the others? Have you seen them?"

She nods absently. "I think they're going to put the couples together."

"That is good." I feel a bit of relief at hearing that. "It will make it easier for us to escape if we are not separated."

"I'm not sure there is an escape," she says, giving her teats another squeeze. "And they put me in here with you."

She speaks as if such a decision is significant, but I am not sure why. I just twist my hands in the ropes again, desperate more than ever to be free. With her presence here, my protectiveness is surging, and I cannot do anything with my hands tied behind my back.

My small movements catch her attention. She focuses on me, and her hand goes to my arm. "Here, I bet I can get those free for you."

"No," I tell her. "I do not wish for you to endanger yourself by helping me..."

My voice dies as she puts her hand on my bare arm and strokes it. A little breathless sound escapes her throat, and she just pets me for a moment, her focus on my arm instead of my bonds.

And I, shamefully, react to this touch. I can feel my cock stiffen in my leathers. Despite the situation, despite the fact we might not live to see another day, despite the fact that this female will flirt with and tease any male, I want her as badly now as I did when I first saw her. My body does not care about any of this—it only realizes that her touch feels good.

"Brooke." I say her name in a thick voice full of warning and question, both.

"Right. Your hands." She makes another soft little noise in her throat that makes my sac tighten, and then her wandering finger-tips move from my arm down to my hands, where she works on my bonds.

"I do not want you to endanger yourself," I try again, but she interrupts.

"Don't think that's gonna be a problem. Trust me." She gives that soft, almost shy chuckle, and I have to bite back my own groan. Why am I reacting so fiercely to her? Why, at such a dangerous time, can I not control my own cock? My thoughts?

Is this...resonance?

I hold my breath and go very still, listening. There is no hum in my body, no song in my khui. It is as silent as ever.

I do not know if this makes me glad or angry.

Freedom first, I remind myself, and concentrate on the light touch of her fingers. She pulls at the strange ropes, and within moments, they loosen about my wrists. I breathe a sigh of relief, pulling my arms forward and then rubbing at my sore wrists. I glance at the door, expecting the guards to charge through.

No one does, so I twist around and begin to untie my feet. Brooke just sits there, watching me. Her hands are tucked under her arms, as if she is hugging herself, and there's a miserable look on her face. My suspicions grow as I finish freeing my legs and no one arrives. Why have they left Brooke with me? How did she know so much about what is happening, and how is she sure that it is safe for me to untie myself? My dislike of her makes me ask, "Are you working with them?"

That soft, shy chuckle escapes her, and the look on her face is wistful. "If I were, do you think I'd be a captive like you?"

I grunt, because this is a truth that cannot be denied. "I am sorry."

"Don't be. We're all on edge." She cups her teats again, and her thumbs stroke over the hard tips through her leathers. "Some of us more than others."

I do not like that she keeps touching herself like that in front of me...or rather, I like it far too much. Those are touches a lover should do to his mate. Touches I want to do to her teats for her. I grit my teeth and move to the entrance of our strange cave, running my fingers along the seams, trying to figure a way to pry it open. "How do we get out?"

"I don't think we can," she tells me. "See that panel? You need a code to get through."

Eh? I glance over at what she's pointing at, but I see nothing but flashing lights set into the stone of the walls. She is human, though, and they know more about such strange things than I do. "So what do we do now, then?"

"We wait." Brooke hesitates, and then gets to her feet. "We find some way to pass the time."

And there is a husky note in her voice that makes my body tighten in response. Before I can ask why she is behaving in such a way, she moves to my side and lifts her arms, putting her hands on my shoulders. I think for a moment she is going to mouth-mate with me, but instead, she moves forward and presses her magnificent teats against my chest.

"Too tall to kiss," she murmurs breathlessly. "Unless you want to lean down and help a girl out."

She is gazing up at me in such a way that it is clear what her interest is. This is the way she looks at others when she wants something from them. This is her flirting, her teasing to get her way.

But I am confused. What is it she can possibly want from me right now? I have no weapon or anything to offer her.

My protection? She will always have that, as a vulnerable female. But perhaps she does not realize this and needs reassurance? "You do not have to put your mouth on mine, Brooke. I will protect you from the others. I will keep you safe."

"That's not it at all," she tells me, and slides her hand down my chest, feeling the protective plates that cover my heart.

I try to remain impassive at such a touch, but my body reacts anyhow. I am going to spill in my pants if she continues this, and I must focus. I need to think of a way to save her, to save the others. The tribe depends on this. I might be the only conscious male right now...

But then Brooke crooks her finger at me, indicating I should lean down.

Fascinated, I do.

5

TAUSHEN

*B*rooke loops her arms around my neck, one hand knotting in my mane. She leans in even closer to whisper in my ear—

Only to bite my earlobe.

I groan in surprise, shocked at both her bold action and the response it elicits in my body. Powerful, hungry need surges through me, and it takes everything I have not to clasp her by the waist, push her to the wall of this strange cave, and shove my hand between her thighs and see if her cunt is wet for me.

It takes a moment for me to realize she is speaking. Whispering. "I have a problem," she tells me in my ear, and then gently sucks on my earlobe.

This time, I cannot stop the groan that erupts from my throat. "Problem?" I breathe, all the blood in my body surging to my cock. "What is it?"

"I think I've been roofied," she tells me, her delicious tongue sliding along my earlobe. And she gives a little sigh as if she is the happiest creature ever. "Your skin tastes amazing."

My skin? All I can think is that her tongue is incredibly smooth and soft and slick against my earlobe, and her little square teeth feel incredible as they nip at me. I try to concentrate on what she is saying. "You...you are rooted?"

"Roofied," she repeats. "I need to have sex. Need to mate."

Is this what "roo-fee" means? She wishes to mate? Now? But when she slicks her small tongue against my ear again, I cannot resist her. I clasp her against me, dragging her body against my hard cock. She gives a low moan and slides one hand there, caressing it. "Now?" I cannot help but ask.

"The aliens want pregnant females," she tells me breathlessly, whispering in my ear. "They think you're my mate. Or that we can be mates. They'll keep us together, I think, but only if you make me pregnant."

I am shocked. She wants me to get her with child? This is why she wants to mate? "I...cannot make you bear a kit," I tell her. "Not without resonance—"

She presses her fingers to my mouth, silencing me. "Don't tell them that. Let them think what they want, as long as it keeps us together. If they think we're mated, they'll keep us together. If not, we're expendable." She gives me another hot look that tells me she is very much still thinking about mating, despite the fact that I cannot give her a kit, and caresses my cock again through my leathers. "I can see you're not totally opposed to the idea," she teases. "How about it?"

"You truly want to mate?"

"I don't know if 'want' to is the right word for it." She gives a little laugh that almost sounds as pained as it is aroused. "More like I need to."

Because she wishes to keep the secret? She wants the aliens to think she is my mate? It seems like a large thing to pretend, but when she caresses my cock again, that soft look in her eyes, I think she might wish to touch me despite the deception.

Cautiously, I lean in and press my mouth lightly to hers. Her mouth is soft, her breath sweet, and she moans with pleasure at the mouth-mating. If this is what she wants—what will keep her safe—how can I refuse? The truth is that her touch excites me, and the thought of mating with her, of taking her as my pleasure-mate, fills me with great joy. It does not matter that our captors are what bring us together. After this, I will keep her in my furs and make her realize that she does not need to flirt with others to get what she wants.

I will be the only one for her. I will tend to all her needs. I will be her male in all ways. She will need no other. She will look at no other. I will be hers and she will be mine, even without resonance. Let Warrek take Suh-mer. I have claimed Brooke as my own in this moment.

"More," she demands, and I eagerly do as she asks. I slant my mouth over hers again, pressing my lips to hers with all the feverish intensity I feel. She makes a frustrated noise in her throat, and her mouth opens under mine. Startled, I realize I am doing it wrong when she slicks her tongue into my mouth. Of course. Her tongue wishes to mate with mine. With a groan, I clasp her against me and give her my tongue. When she makes a little noise of pleasure, I realize this is what she craves. I experiment with what movements she likes, and when I slide my tongue against hers, stroking as I would my cock into her cunt, she makes such noises that I nearly lose control. A mouth-mating, indeed.

Over and over, I mate my tongue with her smooth one, enjoying her sweet taste and her responses. Her body presses against mine, and I cannot help but let my hands roam over her. I caress her rounded bottom, slide my hands along her sides and her hips, and when I can resist no longer, I caress her fascinating rounded teats.

Her moan of encouragement makes my sac tighten against my body, and I close my eyes, breaking from our kiss to control myself. I cannot spill in my pants. I must not. I need to treat her as if she is my mate. She wants to fool the others, and no male would ever spill in his pants at the touch of his female.

If Brooke has noticed that I have paused, she does not care. She makes a frustrated sound in her throat and tears at her leathers, pulling them over her head and revealing a strange band she wears over her teats.

"Undress," she commands me. "Now. Please."

I nod and pause for only a moment. What if our captors are watching? Then, I realize it does not matter—if I want to keep Brooke at my side, I must claim her regardless. Let them see me take my mate, then. Let them watch me claim her. I groan at the thought and rip at the ties to my leathers, yanking them down my legs and then kicking them free. My boots are next, and I strip them off just as fast, eager to touch her more.

Brooke is naked now, as well, her teat-band gone, her leggings and boots tossed aside. Her pale skin is glowing in the strange light, her eyes a vivid khui-blue in her face. She is all pink every-where except for the tuft between her thighs, and I am fascinated by how dark it is in comparison.

"What are you looking at?" she asks, breathless.

"Your cunt has a dark mane," I tell her, and then reach out to brush my fingers over one bouncy, pink-tipped teat. "But you are not dark here."

She moans and moves against me, her arms going around my waist. "That sounds so filthy, and I can't believe how much I like hearing that."

It does? I continue to caress her teat, fascinated by the soft pink tip of it. "How is it filthy?"

"Because you said 'cunt' and 'mane' and 'dark.'" She wriggles up against me, and her voice drops to an even softer, huskier note. "You should have said 'wet' and 'hot' and 'aching,' too."

This time, it is my groan that echoes in the room. "And is it?"

"Oh god, yes."

Since she stroked my cock so boldly, I decide to be as bold with her. I cup her cunt with my hand, letting my fingers play over her mound. She is wet, I realize, and just as warm and inviting as I have imagined. The breath hisses from my throat, and I cannot resist pressing a finger between the folds of her, exploring deeper. "You feel as good as I have imagined."

She clings to my shoulders, moaning and pressing her flat brow to my skin. "Oh, fuck me, have you been thinking about touching me, Taushen?" She wriggles against my hand, as if she wants to mount it like she would my cock, and each movement inflames my need for her.

"Many, many times," I tell her. I can confess all now that she is to be my mate. "I have stroked my cock to your face many a time. I have imagined touching your teats and seeing your reaction. I have imagined what it would feel like to push deep inside you and feel your legs clasp around my waist. Yes, my Brooke, I have thought about claiming you many, many times." I lean in and nip at her small ear, as she did mine. "And it has made me very jealous to see you tease other males to get what you want. You are mine."

She shudders. "That's so fucking caveman of you. Shouldn't make me as hot as it fucking does, but I'm so wet at the thought."

She is. I can feel her slickness all over my hand. I stroke a finger along her folds, feeling for the mysterious third nipple that others have mentioned that human females have. There it is, nestled near the top of her cleft, and when I brush against it, she cries out and pushes herself against my hand, panting. I lick her ear again, and when I find the opening to her core with my fingers, penetrate her. This time, she bears down against me, sinking my fingers deep. She wants more. She wants everything I can give her, and the clench of her cunt is as tight and hot as I ever dreamed.

"Taushen," she pants, her nails dragging over my skin frantically. "You want to do this against the wall? Or on the floor?"

"What pleases you?" I want her to be happy with how I touch her. I want to hear her screams of pleasure.

"Anywhere. Everywhere. Just soon," she begs, grinding her cunt against my palm. "Fast and hard, that's what I need."

"You do not want me to go slow?" I ask, exploring the delicate shell of her ear with my tongue. "You do not want me to part your thighs and lick your cunt until you are screaming?"

"Oh fuck," she cries, her thighs clenching around my hand. "We can go slow next time. Right now I need fast. Fast and hard."

I grit my teeth at that, because she is saying all the things I have dreamed of. Perhaps I am dreaming yet, and I will wake up with my cock in my hands and my leathers wet.

I am not moving fast enough to please my demanding mate,

though. She makes a frustrated sound and rocks against my hand once more, then grabs at my hair and tugs me down for another kiss, this one rougher and more frantic than the last. Her mouth feels as soft and hot as her cunt, and I am lost in the sensation of it until she pulls away from me, panting. "Here," she commands. "Against the wall."

And she pulls away from me and presses her hands against the wall, spreading her legs apart and pushing out her pale, rounded bottom.

And I am...shocked. She wishes me to mount her like this? From behind? But...there is no tail to get in the way, only the rounded sweetness of her flesh. I put a hand on one soft buttock, and then let it slide between her thighs, feeling the wet invitation of her cunt.

Brooke cries out and pushes her bottom out farther, as if she can find my cock and bring it inside her. I am fascinated at the thought of claiming my mate like this, and I do not hesitate longer. I take my cock in hand. It aches with fierce need, the head dripping with slick pre-cum, and drag it along her folds, letting her know I am about to push into her. I do not want to scare her.

But Brooke only gives a fierce "yes" and pushes back against me, rubbing her cunt along the length of my cock.

She feels like nothing I have ever imagined, even in my most heated thoughts, and I cannot resist dragging my length against her folds, over and over again.

"Oh god, you had to have ridges, didn't you?" she chokes out, her little rocking movements along my length maddening. She presses one hand between her thighs, her fingertips grazing my cock-head with every thrust forward I make. "You're going to feel amazing inside me, aren't you?"

"Yes," I tell her thickly. Now she is the one talking "filthy" to me, telling me things that make my cock jerk in response. Does she wish for me to speak such words to her again? "I have ridges and a spur," I tell her. "All for your pleasure."

"Oh, fuck. I forgot about the spur," she breathes, twisting to look over her shoulder at me. "Where does it go when you fuck me like this?"

"We will find out," I tell her, and fit the head of my cock against the entrance to her core. "Are you ready to learn?"

Brooke gives a little shriek that might be a yes, and then she's pushing back against me, encouraging me with her body to plunge forward. I want to, but I go slow instead, watching as my dark blue cock sinks deeper and deeper into her pink, hot, wet flesh. I nearly come at the sight of her cunt gripping my length, clasping it tightly, but I want more than a quick spill inside her. I focus on Brooke instead, concentrating on her reactions and that I am not hurting her. That my thick length is not too much for her smaller body to clasp. That my spur does not stab her uncomfortably as I sink in. That she does not tense in pain or dislike.

But her moans are only ones of encouragement, not discomfort. "Oh, fuck me, your spur…"

I groan, as well. When I sink in fully, the root of my cock flush against her bottom, my spur has sunk deep into the pucker of her bottom, and it feels…indescribable. I stiffen, realizing just how deeply she can clasp all of me.

She writhes against me. "More," she chants. "More, Taushen. Don't stop now."

Stop? Never. I put a hand to her delicate shoulder, then clasp her at the back of her neck, anchoring her in place so my next stroke can be as firm and forceful as she wants. "You like it when I claim you, my mate?"

She gives a little cry. "Oh, fuck yes. Taushen, you filthy thing, you. You're going to claim the hell out of me, aren't you?"

I growl, because her excitement is making mine impossible to contain. I slam into her with my next thrust, and her shudder of delight makes me pound into her again. "I am going to claim your cunt," I rasp between strokes, and when I feel her tighten, quivering, around my cock, I tell her more. "And then I am going to claim your mouth."

"With your cock? God, you're so filthy." She squirms, delighted at my words. "Tell me more."

More? I cast about, thinking. How else can I claim her? What ways have I not thought of? A new idea occurs to me, and I growl low again. "After I claim your mouth, I will push my cock between your teats and claim them, too."

She cries out, a shudder ripping through her. "You're going to fuck my tits?"

"Yes," I tell her firmly, and reach up to clasp one, teasing the tip between my fingers. She arches, crying out loudly, so loud that surely our captors must be hearing such things. "I am going to claim all of you, Brooke. You are mine and mine alone. Understand?"

"Yes," she cries, her fingers clawing at the wall. "Just keep fucking me, Taushen. Yes!"

I do. I give her everything I have, sinking deep into her with every powerful thrust. She clasps me tight, her body quivering with every push into her, and it feels as if she is growing tighter and tighter with every stroke.

But she is frantic, and it is clear she needs more. "Harder," she demands, pressing her cheek against the wall. "Pull my hair."

Pull her hair? I give it an experimental, gentle tug, and she makes a sound of pleasure. "Pinch my tits. Make me come, Taushen. Make me come so hard."

"So demanding," I grit between clenched teeth, fascinated by how wild she is. "Perhaps you should ask me nicely and I will make you come."

"Fuck," she whimpers. "I need to come."

"Then tell me you are mine, and I will make you come," I caress her teat lightly, letting my fingers skim over the tip. She pushes it against my hand, but I go still and she squirms, frustrated.

"Yours," she cries out. "Yours, Taushen. All yours. Now make me come. Please!"

"Tell me what you need." I grasp a handful of her hair again and pull her head back, ever so gentle. "Tell me what you need to make you come, Brooke."

"My clit," she moans. "Touch my clit while you fuck me."

Between her thighs? I nod, and love that she is so demanding. Has any female ever been so strong and so sweetly giving at the same time? I thrust into her again and then slide my hand down her hip to her cunt, seeking out her clit. I drag my fingertips up and down her folds, seeking the right touch, and when I find it, she screams.

I can feel her entire body shudder and quake around me. She tightens, and then I feel her release break over her. Her cry grows low, and she sags against the wall, panting as her cunt clenches over and over again around my cock.

Another growl breaks from my throat, and with a few more

thrusts, I come, too. My release pours forth from my body, and I empty into her as if my lifeblood pours from my body to hers. Still I pump into her, ignoring the fact that my release is draining my strength and that her cunt is filled with my seed, our movements slick.

She is mine. With every thrust inside her, she is mine.

My Brooke. My mate.

6

BROOKE

*O*nce isn't enough.

I realize that through a lust-riddled fog of thoughts as I rest against the wall, trying to catch my breath. That was the most amazing sex I've ever had...and it still wasn't enough. The ache inside me still burns as much as ever, and I whimper at the realization.

This is going to be a long, long night.

Taushen pulls his body free from me, and I can feel our mingled releases wetting the insides of my thighs. I feel hollow from our coming together, and not just because of how big he is. I still ache deep inside. He pulls me against him, his skin sweaty, and he cups my chin with his fingers. "Did I hurt you?"

"No," I answer truthfully. He could have been ten times rougher and I would have eaten up every second of it. "I need more, though."

His eyes widen a little, and he rubs his thumb along my jaw. It takes everything I have not to rub against him like a kitten. "You did not come? I did not please you?"

Oh, I came. And oh boy, he pleased me. "Yes and yes, but I still need more. I'm afraid I'm going to be really demanding for the next while."

He chuckles and leans in, still panting. "Then I shall give you what you need. But my body must have time to recover."

Right. His dick hasn't been roofied. I'm the one suffering. I nod.

He presses a light kiss to my cheek, then the corner of my mouth, and I ache with just how sweet those light caresses are. To think that he could be so rough—on demand, of course—a few moments ago and so incredibly tender now just makes me want him harder. It doesn't hurt that he's easy on the eyes and covered in muscles. I'm still getting used to the horns and tail, but oh god, I'm so not opposed to the spur.

That filthy, filthy spur.

Just thinking about that makes me shudder all over again.

He gives my cheek another caress and then moves away. I want to whine with protest at the loss of his heated skin against mine, but he's picking up his leathers, spreading them out on the floor, and it's obvious he's making us a soft nest to sit on. It's thoughtful, given that this room looks like it's just a storeroom in the ship and there's no place soft to sit and relax. I'm touched at how caring he is, and when he indicates I should sit on the nest he's created, I do so, sinking gratefully onto the leathers. I'm tired but restless at the same time, and it's frustrating. When Taushen sits next to me, I practically fling myself into his arms, burying my face against his neck and inhaling his scent. God save me, even his sweat smells amazing. This roofie is some potent shit. I thought

Taushen was attractive and sexy before, but this thing is bringing me to new levels.

When he doesn't protest my clinginess, I crawl into his lap and straddle him, his half-mast cock tucked between us. I press my breasts against his chest, rubbing up and down so my nipples can tease against his pectorals. He's got ridges everywhere, and I love the tactile feel of him against me. His skin is like suede, not quite furry all over, but that soft chamois feeling that makes him an absolute joy to touch. And then he's got those hard, armored plates that feel something like I imagine a hoof might feel like, but they're ridged and cover his arms and his chest, tapering down to more smooth chamois skin.

And his cock...sigh. Just thinking about his cock makes me all wet and needy again.

"You are whimpering," he murmurs, caressing my face with strong fingers. "Are you cold?"

I shake my head, rubbing my breasts against his chest again. "Not when you're so warm and I can crawl all over you."

He chuckles and his hands slide down my back and rest on my butt. He leans in, and I think he's going to make out with my ear, but he whispers, "Do you think our captors are fooled?"

Oh. I forgot all about them in the heat of the moment. I sink my hand into his thick, almost ropey hair. "I don't know if they need more convincing, but I'm down for round two."

Really, really down.

Taushen sucks in a breath, as if surprised by my suggestion. I'm not sure why—we just had sex. It's not like this is something new. Or is it because I'm so insatiable? Right now I don't even care that the aliens might be watching. Let them watch. I wouldn't care if there was an auditorium filled with people eating popcorn and watching him touch my breasts. All I know is that if I don't get more of him, I'm going to lose my mind.

But then he leans in and puts his mouth on mine again, and I forget about everything. I forget about being drugged. I forget about our captors. I forget about the very real return to slavery I'm facing. I don't need anything but his kiss right now. I lose myself in his touch, fascinated by the ridges on his tongue as it slicks against mine. I need more of everything, and I need it now. I rock against his cock while straddling him, letting him know that I'm ready and willing.

"Shhh," he murmurs, and I realize I'm making those soft whimpering noises again. "We have time. Let me touch you."

Easy for him to say. He doesn't feel like he's being eaten alive by his cravings. But when he begins to gently touch me, exploring me, I close my eyes and relax, trying to focus on how good it feels and not the gnawing need inside me. He caresses me all over, his hands moving across my breasts and my belly, and it feels wonderful. I wrap my arms around his neck even tighter and bury my face against his skin, licking the hollow where his throat meets his shoulder, just below the shock collar. Even his sweat is delicious.

His hand goes between my thighs, and I jerk hard against him, shaking my head. "No, not there." If he tries to finger me or give me oral, I think it'll just make me crazier. I need the real thing.

Taushen pauses, frowning. "You do not wish for my touch?"

"It's too much," I tell him, and lean in to bite at his throat again. I'm frantic, panting. Aching. "I want you deep inside me. No substitutes." And just to add some encouragement, I push my hand between us and grip his cock.

His breath hisses from between his teeth.

"See what I mean?" I tell him between nips at his neck. "Is it too much?"

He growls low in his throat, and his hand tightens on my hips. An aroused pulse of reaction flares in my body. "Then tell me what you want."

"You. Deep inside me. I thought I made that obvious."

There must be something in my tone that sets him off. He gives a short, almost barking laugh, and then surges forward. I barely manage to hold on to his neck, surprised, and then I find myself flat on my back on the pile of leathers, with Taushen's body over me. "Is this what you want?" he demands, and then claims my mouth in a deep, searing kiss.

Oh boy, is it ever. I make a little noise of affirmation and lift my hips, trying to rub against his cock.

This time, there's no more playing around. He pushes one of my thighs forward, practically pressing it to my chest, and then I feel him surge into me.

I gasp, because not only does it feel incredible, but his spur is hitting me right in the most perfect of spots. When he strokes inside me, it rubs against my clit. It is...the best thing ever. *Ever.* I'm officially converted into the spur fan club.

"Is this how you want it, my mate?" he growls as he thrusts into me again. His cock pushes into me so hard that I'm practically seeing stars in the best kind of way.

My cry of delight reverberates in the room. Oh god, is it *ever* what I want. "Yes. Yes!"

He makes a low sound of pleasure, and then he's pumping into me again, leaning forward so hard that my legs are in the air, his weight pressing on my thighs. With every stroke, he pushes deeper into me, and it's the best thing I've ever felt. I claw at his back, screaming with every thrust. When I come again, my body feels as if it's exploding. The intensity between us is staggering, and I'm left gasping for breath as he groans my name, pumping into me. "Brooke," he pants. "Brooke. Brooke."

I marvel at just how well he says my name compared to the other sa-khui, when he gives a little snarl and shudders, his release coming over him. I cling to him, holding tight. We're both damp with sweat, and I'm pretty sure I'm sticky all over, but I'm also exhausted—and that's a good thing.

Maybe this drug—or drink or whatever—has a short-lived window. Whatever it is, I'm relieved when I fall asleep.

7

BROOKE

*W*hen I slowly wake up from my sleep, I find that I'm curled around a large, impossibly warm, blue body. One big hand cups my ass and the other possessively hugs my shoulders. I'm sprawled against a massive chest, and my mouth looks dangerously close to one hard barbarian nipple.

Oh, this is going to get awkward *fast*.

I sit up, squinting at the lights overhead. I wish I had a hangover, or fuzzy memories of last night. Something I could blame impairment on and say that it wasn't me who called Taushen nasty and demanded that he pull my hair.

Nope. I remember it crystal clearly. That was all me. A very aroused, not-my-normal-self me, but still me. Hoo boy.

Taushen reaches out to cup my cheek. "Sleep well?"

I dodge his touch as best I can, faking a yawn. Of course,

stretching my arms makes me aware that I'm still naked. And sore from last night. And Taushen's naked, too. And parts of him are real *happy* to see me awake.

Oh *boy*.

I scrub my hands down my face. "I kind of wish I was still asleep."

"I, too, wish this was a bad dream." He glances at the door, a worried look on his handsome face. Then he gazes back at me, and his expression softens. "Not all of it, though."

"Taushen," I say gently. Oh dear. This is going to be difficult. I hesitate, trying to think of the best way to phrase this.

He sits up, and I notice—totally against my will! Totally!—that he's erect and just as large and ribbed as I remember. "I have been waiting a long time for you to wake up. I hunger to kiss you again."

And there it is. I shrivel a little inside, knowing that this is going to come across really badly. "About last night...we should just forget it ever happened." I glance at the door. "Unless the aliens come back again, then we need to pretend we're mates still."

Taushen stiffens, his glowing eyes narrowing. "Pretend?"

"Yep."

"What do you mean, pretend?"

"You're going to make me clarify, aren't you?" I wrinkle my nose, but I suppose I expected that. "Okay. I thought we were on the same page with the roofie thing."

"You mentioned this word last night. You did not say what it was."

Did he...did he not grasp that part? "You guys know English, though! How can you not know what a roofie is? Better yet, how can you not freaking ask when I say 'Oh, I've been roofied'?"

His jaw clenches slightly. "If I asked every time a human spat a word I did not understand, I would be asking all day long—"

"Oh, dickface!"

"—such as now," he continues. "So no, I did not ask. What is this roo-fee?"

This is not happening to me. I press my hands to my forehead. "I can't believe you never questioned this. Dude, a roofie is when someone gives you something that makes you want to have sex when you don't want to."

He recoils like I've just told him his dick turned into a snake. "You did not wish to mate?"

"Not really? I mean, it wasn't high on my to-do list."

The big lunk just stares at me, shocked. "But you said you wished to mate with me to ensure that our captors thought we were resonance mates."

"I did say that." I twist my hands, feeling awkward and horrible. Did any chick ever have to explain to her one-night stand that this wasn't a forever thing? Gah. It'd be so much easier if I could just grab my shoes and run for the nearest elevator. Unfortunately, there's no getting away. "I also said 'pull my hair' and 'fuck me, you nasty thing' and stuff like that. What I'm trying to say is that I wasn't exactly myself. And we probably could have pretended to be mates just by, you know, holding hands and stuff." I drop my voice to a whisper and glance at the door again, as if expecting orange aliens to be peeping at us even now.

"You put your hand on my cock and bit me." He looks indignant.

"I didn't say I was a good girl! I said I was roofied. There's a difference. It takes away any inhibitions."

"You...did not wish to mate?"

He's finally getting it. "No. I'm sorry."

The look on his face becomes slowly horrified. "Because you were not thinking clear. Because they made you take something that made you want to mate."

"Bingo."

Taushen's nostrils flare, and he jerks to his feet, stalking the four corners of the room. He paces back and forth, silent, but his tail twitches madly, and I can tell he's really upset. As for me, I'm not sure how I feel. I don't feel violated like I thought I would. I don't think the roofie was strong enough or mentally impairing enough. I do remember everything. But I do feel weird about things. Like I drank too much at the bar and took someone home I didn't intend to, and now he won't leave. Yeah, that's the best way to describe this. As plans go, it wasn't a bad plan. Shack up, have some dirty sex to make our captors think we're together, and then let the chips fall where they may.

Except Taushen's chip has fallen firmly in the "mated" category and I can tell he's having a hard time realizing that I'm not going to be his little woman. He keeps glancing over at me, and there's agony in his eyes.

And shit, I feel *bad*. I shouldn't, because I'm the victim here, but I should have stopped to make sure he knew what a roofie was. I should have said it was just for fun when he was all calling me his "mate" and stuff instead of demanding that he fuck me harder. We're both to blame for assuming things.

He looks over at me and then snatches up his leathers from the floor and hands me mine. "You should dress."

"Oh. Right." I grab my tunic, and for some reason, his reaction makes me feel dirty. "Look, Taushen, I'm sorry things turned out the way they did—"

"Sorry?" He bites out the word, again both shocked and angry at my reaction. "You should not be *sorry*. They gave you something that made you want me." His hands clench. "I want to rip their throats out."

My eyes widen. "Um, okay. Me too."

He clenches and unclenches his hands again. "To think they would do such a thing to a female." He shakes his head slowly, and I watch his jaw clench. I can practically hear his teeth gritting together.

"They don't care," I tell him quietly. "To them, we're little more than livestock. They're going to breed us and sell us. At least like this, we're together and not sold separately." At least until they figure out that he can't make me pregnant without resonance, but I hope that won't come up anytime soon. I pull the tunic over my head.

When I emerge from my clothes, Taushen moves to sit next to me. "Are you all right? Did I hurt you?" His gaze roams over me, and the look on his face is worried. "I was not gentle."

"I'm okay. Maybe in a few days it'll all hit me and I'll freak out, but right now I'm okay." I give him a brave smile. "Until then, we need to figure out what we're going to do."

"You and I are going to—" He pauses and jumps to his feet again.

The door opens and the aliens enter. They're holding the long, strange-looking rods that serve as their guns, and one makes that weird wheezing sound I know is a laugh when he looks over at me.

Taushen just snarls and lunges for the nearest alien, a murderous look on his face. Hands outstretched, he manages to grab the clothing of the first one before the shock collar lights up and he slumps to the ground.

I bite back the scream rising in my throat and watch, horrified, as he twitches on the floor, unable to move. The aliens just laugh again. I crawl to his side and put his head in my lap, because that seems like something a mate would do. Plus, it's kind of sweet of him to defend my honor.

Maybe he's not such an awful guy after all. He sure wasn't an awful lay.

Not that I'm thinking about that sort of thing.

One of the aliens squats on the floor next to me. He tilts his head and gives me a toothy smile. "Yoooouuuu will not trrrryy saaaame, no?"

I shake my head, stroking one of Taushen's horns. "No," I say quietly.

"Tellllll ussss...howwww mannny moooorrrr?"

How many more? Is he asking about Warrek and Summer? Nervous, I force myself to focus on Taushen's face. His eyes are closed, and his horns seem impossibly big from this angle, his hair thick and falling over my lap like a waterfall. Do I tell the truth? Do I lie? What's the right thing to do here? "No others," I say after a moment. "Just us."

"Howwww...youuuu...arriiiiive heeere?"

How did we get here? How did we arrive? "We are slaves," I tell him, deciding that half-truth is all I've got. I try to think of a story that covers everyone, including pregnant Harlow and the other women, and how sa-khui and human got mixed. "We...had an old master and he set us free here when he died." Er, sure. Seems legit.

The alien studies me and then tangles one of his lobster-claw fingers in my pink hair. "Iffff...youuuu lieee..."

The threat is unspoken. I swallow hard. "Not lying." Totally lying.

As I watch, Taushen—who I thought was unconscious—raises a hand slowly and reaches for the throat of the alien leering at me.

This time, I feel the sizzle they send through his body thanks to our shared contact, and we both go unconscious.

8

BROOKE

*W*hen I wake up, we're alone, and Taushen's in a bad mood. Some chewy, awful ration bars of some kind have been left, along with two drink boxes of water, and I eat and drink my share, trying to be calm. I've been in a situation like this before. I know what to expect, and I'm going to need my strength.

Taushen just paces, back and forth, back and forth. His tail flicks wildly as he does. Every conversation I try to start goes nowhere, so I eventually give up and nap.

Time passes. I don't know how long we're locked up. The room we're in doesn't have a clock, and the lights remain on all the time. I sleep fitfully, and Taushen just paces. If he naps, it's when I'm asleep. Food continues to be left for us, and the aliens come by to quiz me again some time later. This time, they don't touch my hair, just ask me how many others are out there.

And they don't look happy with my answer, which makes me wonder what's going on.

There's not much to do in the cell, especially since Taushen isn't talking anymore. So I fiddle with my hair, braiding it back and forth. Fishtail braid, French braid, four-strand braids, Dutch braids, anything I can think of. My hair isn't all that long, so I have to get creative and use small sections. Taushen's hair is better than mine, and I'm itching to braid it, but every time I make the suggestion, he just shoots me an angry look and goes back to pacing.

It feels like days are passing, but maybe I'm wrong. Maybe it's only been one day and I'm just so stir-crazy it feels like more.

I'm picking apart my latest braid when the door opens. Taushen and I immediately jerk to alertness, and he steps in front of me protectively, baring his sharp teeth at them.

One alien raises his gun at Taushen, as if daring him.

Taushen starts to take a step forward, but I put a hand on his ankle, a silent plea for him not to. If he gets knocked out again, it doesn't help either of us. He pauses, and then, snarling, takes a step back.

They gesture he should move aside.

Taushen doesn't. He continues to stand in front of me, an army of one.

"It's okay," I tell him softly. "Don't get yourself killed over me. I'm not worth it."

This time, his angry gaze is focused on me, and he stalks away a few feet to glower from afar.

One of the aliens moves to squat next to me on the floor. "Haaaannndd."

Ugh, is he checking to see if I'm pregnant? I consider telling him the truth, that I know I'm not pregnant, but that seems stupid after all I've been through. I obediently hold my hand out and only wince a little when he sticks me with his gauge.

"No...conceptionnnn," he says. "Youuuu are not tryyyying harrrd enoughhh."

I'm about to protest when the other makes that wheezing sound. Oh, a joke. Great. I suppose that answers whether or not they noticed Taushen and I having sex. My guess is that they did. I just keep a smile pasted to my face and pretend like I didn't understand the question. "What do you mean?"

But he changes tactics on me. The look on his face grows angry. "Therrrr arrr moooorrr of youuuu," he says, his words practically garbled in his haste to spit them out. "Youuuu lieeee."

Oops. Well, too late to change stories now. I blink my eyes innocently and twirl a piece of my hair. "I have no idea what you're talking about. You captured everyone I know of."

His face tightens and for a moment, I think he's going to slap me. Instead, he pulls something out of his pocket. I recognize that bottle. "Do yuuuu waaaannnntt thisssss?"

I glance at it and then back at him. It's clear that he knows I don't. "Not...really?"

"Thennnn talllkkk."

They're going to roofie me again unless I do what they ask. A small whimper escapes my throat at the thought, because I don't want that. I want to be able to choose my own adventure, damn it.

Taushen growls with rage, and the alien brandishes his gun again. Taushen's collar lights up, and it's clear that it's a warning. Just try it.

Except I know Taushen's man enough to try it again. I know he'll do anything to keep me safe, and the thought is weirdly comforting. I don't want him to get hurt, but the thought that he's willing to go that far to protect me does a lot for my mental state. I can be brave. I can.

"Whoooo issss outtt therrrrr?" my alien captor asks again, waving the bottle at me in a threat.

I swallow hard. I can be brave. I can. "No one."

He snarls low and mutters something to his companion. To my surprise, Taushen drops to his knees, groaning as a shock rips through him.

I gasp. "What are you doing?" But I know—they're using him against me. They want me to talk, so they're going to torture Taushen in the hopes that I'll break. For some reason, it's easier to think of being hurt myself than someone being tortured on my behalf. I can't handle it. "Don't, please!"

The two aliens pause, their round, fishlike eyes on me. "Whaaaat doooo yooooouuuu knowwww?" one hisses at me. "Speeeeeak."

"There's a hundred of us," I lie quickly. "Lots of them waiting outside to take you down. You guys don't stand a chance."

The alien barks something, clearly seeing through my lie. He reaches forward and grabs me by the throat with his claw-like hand, tilting my head back as he raises the bottle. Me and my big mouth. Fuck. The alien squeezes my lips open by pressing on my jaw, but before he can pour the hated liquid down my throat, Taushen gives a cry of rage and flings himself across the room—and onto the other alien.

Out of the corner of my eye, I see the two of them tumble to the ground. Taushen's larger body is all but covering the slaver, and they both twist on the ground. I can't tell if Taushen's been zapped and just landed lucky or if they're truly fighting. The alien holding me hisses and then releases me. He gets to his feet, lifting his weapon.

Something sizzles in the air, and he collapses.

Everything goes quiet for a moment, and then Taushen flips onto his back. I think for a moment that he's gone down, but to my surprise, he has the other alien pinned in front of him, one big arm across the enemy's throat as the creature flails, gun useless in his hands. There's another sizzle in the air, and the alien goes limp. Taushen blinks, surprised, and then looks at me.

I raise my hands. "I didn't do it—"

"I did." A familiar voice comes from the hallway, and I see a big blue body with long, silky black hair enter the room.

Warrek. He's got one of the aliens' guns tucked under his arm, and he offers a hand out to Taushen. Taushen takes it and jumps to his feet, then jerks, shuddering a little, and when Warrek releases him and then shakes out his hand, I realize Taushen's still getting shocks sent through him.

And yet he did all that because he thought I was in danger.

"You have my thanks, Warrek," Taushen grits out, tugging at his collar. "How did you get here?"

"Suh-mer," he says simply, and then turns around and leaves, readying his gun once more. Somewhere else in the ship, I can hear Summer yelling at someone and the sound of more sizzling gunfire.

I feel weak with relief. We're being rescued. I move closer to Taushen, because for some reason, I really want a hug right now.

Or for him to put his arms around me and reassure me that we're safe. I need...something.

He stares at me for a long moment, his expression unreadable.

I lean in, trying to slide my arms around his waist.

Taushen gently pushes me away. "I do not trust your touches, Brooke. Not when you are not yourself."

"They didn't drug me this time," I protest, but he shakes his head again. Anger explodes through me, anger and hurt that he would turn me away when I need him. "Well, fuck you, too! I don't want you to touch me, either."

And I keep telling myself that.

WE'RE RESCUED ALL RIGHT. Summer's ridden in and saved the day like a tiny, breathless, Asian badass, guns blazing. She and Warrek had this crazy plan to draw out our captors one by one, and between them and Mardok sabotaging the old ship from within, we were able to get free. Everyone's looking at Summer as if she's amazing, and they're giving me suspicious looks.

I guess I deserve those. After all, I blabbed about families and babies to the aliens, and I nailed Taushen. Taushen, who's ignoring me now that the others are around and acting as if we're back to our normal cold dislike of each other. Fine then. Feeling's mutual.

Except when it's not, like right now. I'm just stewing in hurt.

Turns out that my grand plan of keeping families together didn't do any good. I find out later that all of the couples were kept separated...except me and Taushen. Great. So my big plan only got me screwed. Literally.

But at least Summer and Warrek saved us from slavery. Now I just have to repair the relationships here and go on with my life like everything's okay.

I've picked myself up off the floor before. I can do so again.

9

BROOKE

Present Day

"*D*rink," *a hissing voice tells me, and orange hands grip my throat.* "*Drink!*"

I wake with a start, gasping.

I'm alone. There's no one in my room with me. No orange aliens shoving laced drinks down my throat, no slave collar, no nothing. The room I'm in is empty, my furs spread out on the floor next to the bed. After weeks of sleeping on the ground, the strange bed feels too mushy, too weird. I push the furs off my sweaty skin, shivering.

Just a bad dream.

I wish Taushen was here. His big body would be perfect to snuggle up against until the bad dreams went away.

Of course, then I want to kick myself for thinking such a thing. Taushen hates me. He's been cold to me ever since the rescue, as if I'm to blame for our situation.

Which, okay, I kind of am to blame. I'm the reason we got thrown in together like we were mates. But I had good intentions. I never meant to hurt his feelings, and after what we shared, to not even be friends? Or to get along like normal human beings that have to live in a very, very small tribe together? It sucks.

I lie back in the furs again, but I can't sleep. Every time I close my eyes, I see that orange hand reaching for my throat. With a sigh, I fling the covers back and get to my feet. The door to my room is open—Mardok didn't want any of us accidentally locking ourselves into the ship, so the "door open" sequence has been set permanently —and I head down the hall toward the room that's set up as a cafeteria. It's funny how some things are so strange and space-agey on this ship, but they still have basic things like a medical bay and a kitchen. It's been days and we've been cleaning up the mess the slavers left, and now the ship is clean and tidy, free of the blood that spattered the walls, but it still doesn't feel cozy. Doesn't feel like home. It feels...well, kind of like an office building would feel. Cold. Uninviting.

I can't imagine how Mardok lived here for years. I'd have gone nuts.

Of course, I'm not the only one up. I enter the kitchen area to find Harlow sitting at one of the uncomfortable, sa-khui-sized benches, a strange-looking drinking vessel in her hands. The scent of hot tea is in the air. She looks exhausted, dark hollows under her eyes, and her belly looks enormous in her loose leathers. She manages a wan smile at the sight of me. "Can't sleep?"

"Nope. Nightmares."

"Me too. Want some tea? You have to drink it out of this thing, though." She holds the strange thing aloft, and it looks more like a gravy boat...or a smile—with no handles. "I can't promise you won't spill it all over yourself. I already have twice." She gives me a wry smile. "I miss my favorite cup, but it's back on the other ship, and it seemed silly to send Rukh to go get it."

"Tea sounds great." Better than going back to bed.

She gets up, waddling, and heads to the counter, pressing a few buttons and adding a sprinkle of herbs to one of the strange cups. "It's so strange to have a ship with parts that actually work when you hit the controls," she tells me with a little smile.

"I wouldn't know, I don't know how to use any of this stuff. I just try not to press anything." I get up and take the cup from her, because it seems strange to have a pregnant lady waiting on me. She's right, though. The mug's hard to hold with no handle, and the inside of the cup is inversely domed, so it doesn't hold all that much liquid. So strange. I take a sip, and the tea tastes familiar, at least. It's bitter and strong, like all the sa-khui tea, but I've grown accustomed to it and think of it as having my coffee black. Not that we have coffee. I peek at Harlow over my cup. "So you can't sleep, either?"

"Nope." She sits down again, her feet dangling like a child on the strange, oversized bench. "Too much to think about." She rubs her hand over her face again and looks so pale and exhausted that I worry.

"Like Rukhar?" I ask, thinking of her small son.

Harlow shakes her head violently. "I'm trying not to think about him at all, because if I do, I know I'm going to start crying and, well..." She pauses and sniffs, staring at the ceiling. "I'm thinking about other things instead. Like what if these slavers were working with another crew on another ship, and they're going to come looking for them? Or what if there's a tracker or a beacon somewhere on the ship that we haven't found and it's sending out signals? What if there's an intergalactic check-in somewhere that I don't know about or don't know to ask Mardok, and someone's coming looking for a missing ship? What do we do then?" She sighs and holds her mug tight with both hands. "And then there are the smaller worries, like what are we going to do with twenty new people, and what about all this technology on this ship that's now ours, and the guns, and how do we handle how those things are going to change our world?" Her smile is weak. "You know, 'small' worries."

I snort, enjoying the rush of steam from my cup on my face. "Doesn't feel like a small worry to me. Those are legit things, and it's normal to worry. Look at how everyone reacted to Kate's kitten, and it's just a cat. But you'd think she'd somehow conquered Everest by bringing one into camp. A lot of stuff is new to these guys."

"A lot. Mardok comments on that, too. He's struggling right now because he misses his friends." Her mouth droops a little. "And Farli doesn't know how to help. To her, being murdered for your ship is inconceivable. She can't grasp it, just like most of the sa-khui don't really get it. So it's hard for Mardok to unload. I worry about him. He's working frantically on this ship and..."

"And you don't know what it means for us," I guess. "Or if it's even a good idea."

"I just think that the sa-khui are a good, pure people, you know? They don't need technology or us humans crapping them up with our ideas like stealing and murdering and slavery. I worry we're going to ruin them." The expression on her face grows wistful, and I suspect she's thinking about her mate. There's something a little...untamed about Rukh. A little feral. I prefer my guys like Taushen, a little hot and cold, maybe, but not quite so savage.

Of course, then I could kick myself for thinking about Taushen. "It's rough right now," is all I say, and drink more of my tea.

She nods, the distant look still on her face. After a moment, she focuses on me and puts a hand on the big table between us. "I just want you to know I don't have any hard feelings about what happened here."

A knot forms in my throat. "Oh?"

"At first I thought you were selling us out. I admit I had some... unpleasant thoughts about you for a few days." She grimaces. "Then I realized that you kept emphasizing families and babies to the aliens, and I realized you were trying to do what you could to keep us all together. I appreciate it, and I wanted you to know that. Losing my boys would have gutted me."

"I tried to suggest mated pairs," I tell her, relieved she caught on. "Though I should have grabbed a gun and started blasting, like Summer did." I'm still amazed at my friend. Who knew she was such a spitfire?

"You did what you could," Harlow tells me as I take another sip of my tea. She looks thoughtful. "I just can't figure out why they put you and Taushen together."

Her expression is innocent—overly so—and it takes everything I have to choke my tea down without coughing. I manage to shrug my shoulders and sputter, "Wishful thinking on their part."

"I guess so. He doesn't seem like he was happy with your arrangements." Harlow grimaces. "That must have made it a long few days. Long for everyone, of course, but I can't imagine being trapped with someone that miserable."

"Mmm." I'm suddenly not all that thirsty anymore. Is she right? Does Taushen hate me?

"It's so weird," Harlow says with a little shake of her head. "He used to be so happy. Kind of like a puppy, you know? All eager and ready to take on the world."

"He was?" I'm shocked. I picture Taushen and "puppy-like" isn't what I imagine. "Salty" and "cranky" maybe, but definitely not "puppy." "When?"

"Back when we first arrived. I wasn't in Georgie's original group, but I was one of the six pulled from pods, like our sleeping beauties here." She gestures in the direction of the cargo bay. "I remember Taushen was younger then. About Sessah's age."

I think of Sessah, who's just lanky enough to be in his teen years. He's not filled out like Taushen, nor does he have the broad chest and shoulders and deep, booming voice. I try to picture Taushen like Sessah. I try to picture Taushen giddy and eager like a puppy.

Nope. Can't do it. "So what happened?"

"I don't know." She shakes her head. "Something over the seasons, I guess. I don't recall a single huge incident that would have changed him, like the cave-in. Warrek lost his father then, and he grieved, but his personality didn't change. Taushen's just grew...more unhappy as time passed. It's a shame. He deserves something good in his life, you know?" She gives me a regretful little smile. "It's the mom in me now, I guess, but I keep seeing how miserable he is and wishing something would cheer him up."

Well, now I feel completely guilty. I think of our nasty, filthy, wall-banging round of sex. And then the next one. And him being all possessive and calling me his mate. And then me waking up the next morning and telling him I didn't want to do any of that.

I push my tea away, my stomach in knots. Maybe I should talk to him. Just let him know that I don't blame him for what happened and ask to be friends again. Maybe we can start over without the whole hair-pulling and biting. I don't hate the guy. I don't even hate the situation we were forced into—I've made poor choices in sex partners in the past, and Taushen was the best I've ever had (though maybe that was the roofie talking). As situations go, it wasn't ideal, but it could have been worse.

A horrible thought occurs to me—what if that was Taushen's first time?

What if I de-flowered the guy and then acted like he was dirt the next morning?

Ah, jeez. Things just get more and more complicated the more I think about it.

"Har-loh!" A strident voice breaks the quiet that falls between us.

"Uh oh," Harlow says, and slides to her feet. "I'm in here, Rukh," she calls out. "Keep your voice down. Everyone's still sleeping."

A moment later, a wild-eyed sa-khui hunter tears into the kitchen area. Rukh's hair is a mess around his face, as if he's just woken from sleep, and he's naked. Yikes. I discreetly avert my eyes, even though I know it's not a big thing for the sa-khui. I'm still not used to seeing big blue junk—and spur—hanging out for all the world to see.

"You were gone," he says thickly, striding across the room and pulling Harlow into his arms. I watch discreetly from the corner of my eye as he holds her tight against him, stroking her hair. "I woke and you were gone."

"I'm here," she replies, her voice gentle. "I just wanted a drink, and I stopped to talk to Brooke. Nothing's wrong."

He touches her stomach and then her face, and the wild fear is still in his eyes.

"It's okay," she whispers, and then glances back to me, smiling apologetically. "Brooke and I can finish talking in the morning. 'Night."

"'Night, you two," I say, and drink my cold tea as they leave. I guess I'm not the only one that needs to unpack everything that happened while we were captive. I think of Mardok, who lost all his friends and old crew with the violent takeover. Of Harlow and Rukh, who had to send their son away.

But Mardok has Farli to hold him throughout the night. And Rukh has Harlow to help him through things.

And Taushen hates me.

I sigh, rinsing my weird mug and placing it back on a shelf. I really need to talk to him in the morning. If nothing else, we can come to terms with what happened between us and support each other. There's no need for things to get ugly or unpleasant, or even awkward. Gail and Vaza aren't official, and I'm sure if they broke up...

I pause, because no, I'm wrong there. Gail might be okay if she broke up with Vaza, but Vaza's clearly over the moon when it comes to Gail. Losing her would break him.

Maybe that's the problem here. Maybe these guys don't know how to loosen their grip on a girl. All they know how to do is hold tight.

Of course, I never get the chance to talk to Taushen, because the next morning, the rest of the tribe arrives.

10

TAUSHEN

I search each face of my tribesmates as they arrive. Rokan, who is mated to Li-lah. Bek, who is mated to Ell-ee. Vektal, who is mated to Shorshie. Raahosh and his mate, Leezh. Salukh. Ereven. Hassen. Zolaya. Pashov. Cashol. All mated hunters.

There is no one that can resonate to Brooke. I am relieved, even though I am also angry at myself for being so possessive. She has made it clear she does not wish to be mine. That she only endures my touch when she is drugged.

She is not mine...but I am glad she will also not be another's. Not yet.

Then I think of the four males waiting in their pods and scowl to myself.

Vektal claps me on the shoulder in greeting as they arrive at the cave-ship. The others are close behind, Rokan and Bek pulling up the rear. They drag sleds behind them, full of furs and gear that will be needed. When I see that, I know the answer that my chief has decided.

Like it or not, we will be waking up the twenty strangers.

My distaste for this must show on my face, because Vektal's smile of greeting turns to a concerned look. "Has anything else happened? Have more returned?"

"All is well enough," I tell him, carefully hiding my feelings. "No others have arrived. Come. The others will be glad to see you."

Someone puts a hand to his mouth and calls out a boisterous "ho" in greeting. Zolaya, who is always happy and cheerful. It seems almost inappropriate, though I would not say such a thing. Zolaya has a good heart.

One by one, others emerge from the ship. Rukh appears, spear in hand, and then Farli rushes out to hug her brothers. Mardok follows behind his mate, though his greeting is not as cheery, and Har-loh waits by her mate's side. Brooke does not rush out to greet the others either, taking her time to appear. When she does, I frown to see that her soft mane is knotted in high, decorative tails over each shoulder. Has she made herself attractive knowing that the others would arrive?

Why do I care? Why do I notice? She hates my touch.

"Everyone is well?" Vektal asks, going around to greet each tribes-mate with a clasped arm and a quick look-over. "I wanted to bring Maylak, but the healer said she would be of more use back at Croatoan. The ship can heal just as well as her, she says." He looks dubious. "Is anyone wounded?"

"We are all whole," Farli tells him, casting a worried look at Mardok.

"Only our hearts are bruised," Har-loh says a moment later, and clasps her hands over her belly. "Is Rukhar okay? Did he make the trip all right? Did he cry?" She sounds as if she will cry, as well, and Rukh puts a protective arm around his mate's shoulders.

"Little Rukhar has not left Shail's side," Cashol offers. "He follows her like a shadow, and she clucks over him like a lonely dirtbeak."

"There's a visual," Har-loh says with a teary little laugh and wipes at her eyes. "But it makes me feel a little better, at least."

"Then I am glad." He smiles patiently at her, and I suspect he sees a little of his own mate in Har-loh's tears. "Is there somewhere to set a fire and make tea? I can tell you about Rukhar as we do."

"There's a kitchen," she says, glancing at Rukh and then nodding at Cashol. "I'll show you."

Rukh follows behind them, his hand on Har-loh's back protectively. I see that small move and think, *I understand you.* Cashol is mated, but I understand being possessive of a female. I thought I understood it when I sought Ti-fa-ni's attention many seasons ago. Or when Li-lah and her sister arrived. Or when Farli came of age and there were not many male hunters left unmated in the tribe and I was sure to be her choice for a pleasure-mate. But how I felt all those times pales to how I feel about Brooke now. There is a hungry, furious craving for her deep in my gut that will not ease. I watch her as she greets the others, smiling politely and laughing at Zolaya's jokes as the sleds are parked in the snow nearby.

It does not matter that she is not mine in her eyes. I view her as mine and mine alone.

Vektal claps a hand on my shoulder, drawing my attention. "Show me these new humans," he tells me.

"You just got here," Mardok says. "Want to take a load off first?"

"I have no load that I cannot shoulder," Vektal tells him with a nod, and for some reason that makes Mardok smile. Vektal continues. "And I have thought about these new humans for many, many days. I would wait no longer."

"Come," I tell him. "I will show you."

I turn to go inside the ship and I am not entirely surprised that everyone chooses to follow behind us. Of course they will. It is exciting to hear that new humans will be joining us, even if the others are already mated.

Perhaps I should be excited at the prospect of sixteen new females, all of whom I could resonate to the moment they emerge from their sleep pods. But the thought does not fill me with the joy it would have, once. Instead, I think of Brooke. Brooke, who clung to me even as I thrust into her, crying out her pleasure. Brooke, who bit at my earlobe as if she could not resist a taste.

Brooke, who had been given something by our captors to make her act in such a way.

My stomach curdles at the thought.

It feels strange to be leading my chief in to see the sleeping humans, but Mardok and Farli seem content to follow behind, and Rukh and Har-loh have disappeared. I suppose I must be the one to show them, then. Brooke watches me, too, and it is her gaze that adds a little strength to my step. Perhaps I imagine the approval I see in her eyes. It does not matter. Right now, all that matters is the chief's decision.

I take him to the large, cavernous room in the ship that the others call "cargo bay." The strange pods are lined up along the walls and in a row across the floor, and I lead the group to the first one. The lids are kept over the pods because Mardok and Har-loh fear they will get damaged and wake the sleeping occupant, so I pry the lid off the first one and step back so my chief can see.

Someone jostles me from behind, desperate to peer inside. Vektal leans over, and then frowns, curious. "What is this creature? Is it a human?" He looks to Brooke. "Buh-brukh? Do you have people that look like this?"

She moves to my side, her hand grazing my arm as she moves forward to look at the sleeping male. I am fascinated by that small touch, my cock surging in response. I barely notice her words as she tells the chief that no, that male is not human. She doesn't know what it is. Standing in front of me, her pink-and-brown braids are just below my chin. If I pull her against me, she would fit perfectly against my body. If I inhale deeply, I can breathe in her scent—

"That's a fucking lizard-man and you think he might be human?" Leezh's loud thoughts burst through my fantasy. "Has a third resonance to Georgie squeezed your brain out of your dick?" The yellow-haired human peers over the sleeping male and then gives the chief another disgusted look. "He's got fricking scales. He's bronze. What part of that screams 'human'?"

Raahosh puts a calming hand on his mate's shoulder, mouth twitching with silent amusement. "Perhaps he is not the only one that is sleep deprived. You are yelling, my mate."

"Am I? Shit. Sorry." She grimaces. "I'm just...damn, dude. A friggin' lizard-man? What does that say about what you think we look like?" She casts another disgruntled look in the chief's direction.

"My Shorshie is beautiful beyond anything." Vektal scowls, irritated with Leezh's abrasive words. "I did not mean—"

"He looks a little human, doesn't he, Taushen?" Brooke comments, interjecting. Her voice is sweetly teasing. "If you ignore the scales, he looks a lot more like human people than sakhui people. I can see the mistake."

"He's gold," Leezh says. "And scaly."

"The males are all non-humans, and all the females are humans. I think it kind of goes along with what we've seen of the slavers, but who can guess the reasoning behind selling four alien guys, too?" Brooke continues, and turns toward me. She touches my arm, and my skin feels on fire with that caress. "Can you show Vektal the other males while everyone looks at this one?"

She acts as if we are a team, she and I. I like it far more than I should, and find myself eager to do her bidding. When Vektal looks expectantly at me, I nod and gesture to a pod on the far side of the room. Brooke moves next to Leezh and speaks quietly, the flirty tone in her voice. It is the tone she uses when she wants something, and when Leezh laughs a moment later, I realize she is trying to distract the others so I can show the chief privately. Brooke glances over at me and then points at something else in the scaly male's pod, again using her teasing voice.

It takes me a moment to realize she did not use such a tone on me. Pride puffs my chest. I stride a bit more confidently to the other creature's pod and pull back the lid. "This one is ugly and fierce-looking," I tell him. "I worry he will be a problem when he awakens. The other two males are more human-looking, but Brooke assures me that they are not."

Vektal glances down at the male creature, a twitch in his cheek the only outward sign he has seen it. "What are your thoughts, Taushen? I would hear from you, away from Leezh. She has had many, many things to say this trip and has made clear to me that I should hear her opinion on all of them."

I laugh at that. Leezh has never been shy about voicing her thoughts. I picture the chief hiking, Leezh chattering in his ear about how she thinks things should go with the newcomers, and imagine that Vektal's patience must be strained in this moment. "She has very...firm ideas."

Vektal grunts. "And some of them are good. I do listen...but sometimes I appreciate quiet." He crosses his arms over his chest and gazes down at the sleeping male, a troubled flash crossing his face. "I fear quiet is something we will be losing very soon."

His thoughts echo mine. I worry that it will be a bad thing to awaken these strangers, yet how can we not? I think of Brooke and Li-lah and all of the others that have arrived. They have brought so much joy and life to our small tribe. How can we let them remain asleep? Yet at the same time... "These newcomers worry me."

Vektal nods. "And me as well, but we do not have many choices. They are people, and as people, we must take care of them."

He is not wrong...and yet, I wonder who will take care of my people if these are bad ones? The last people we met were violent and had bad intentions. Our people were not safe with them. I glance over at Brooke, and she has her head tilted, her smile a charming one as she teases Hassen and Pashov about missing their mates. Who will protect Brooke?

I tried to do so once, and I failed. Instead, I hurt her. I took what she did not freely offer.

I will not fail her again, I vow. No matter what is decided with these strangers, she is mine to protect, even if she does not want my protection. I can do no less.

11

TAUSHEN

*V*ektal says no more about the sleepers as one by one, each pod's lid is pried off and the occupant revealed. He remains silent about them even as the group disperses, exploring the ship and making camp. There's not enough room for everyone to stay inside the strange cave-ship—and I suspect that many are uneasy at doing so. I do not blame them. I still do not sleep well most nights, imagining that one of the strange, orange-skinned aliens will appear and steal Brooke and the rest of my tribe away. I suspect that Rukh has the same thoughts I do, because we end up keeping watch silently together most nights, staring out into the snows.

The tribe sets up tents at the base of the ramp, and I watch, gritting my jaw when empty ones are set up and supplies placed inside. I do not have to ask who the empty tents are for. I can guess...and I do not like it.

I keep thinking of Brooke. Her ornate, pretty braids this day. Her laughing, playful expression as she speaks with Pashov or Vektal. I wonder if she will resonate to the gold, scaly male, or the beastly one. Or the two that are not quite human, but look human enough to my untrained eye. Or if she will resonate to no one, condemned to the same lonely fate I am.

None of these thoughts eases me. Surely Brooke is a female worthy of having a mate...and yet I do not wish for her to resonate to any of these males. Just the thought makes me grit my teeth and sets my tail to lashing. But would I not wish for her to be happy?

I think on this, and I have no answer.

A bonfire is built at the end of the ramp, amid the nest of tents, and tea is heated. A fresh kill is divided, raw, amongst the tribe, and Har-loh nibbles on trail rations while both Leezh and Brooke choose to eat their food as we do. I am oddly pleased to see how brave Brooke is in regard to her meal. I know of human females that still refuse to eat their meat raw, and they have been with us for many seasons. Brooke has only been here for one turn of the moon, and already she is working to fit in. She will be a good mate...to someone.

The thought makes my gut clench with jealousy once more.

As the tribe gathers, Vektal gets to his feet. The expression on his face is weary and he looks out at us, as if still weighing his decision up until this moment. His gaze rests heavy on Mardok for a long breath, and then he speaks. "You all know why we are here. And by now, you should know my decision. It is not an easy one to make, because I know that any change we bring changes everything for the entire tribe, not just one or two people. I have weighed this, and I have thought carefully about such things. I have spoken with my mate, and she agrees that we only have one choice we can make, as people. We must open the pods and welcome these strangers into our tribe."

"You know how I feel about this," Bek says, his voice flat. "I do not agree. I do not think we should put our mates and the tribe at risk for people we do not know."

"I agree," I say, getting to my feet. "You were not here when the strangers arrived. They had strong weapons. They took down our fiercest hunters with a mere flick of the wrist. We were lucky to escape them, and we should take this lesson we have learned and remember that not all people are friendly people." I want to look in Brooke's direction, but I dare not. "That they do not view us in the same light that we view them."

"But how can we leave them as they are?" Zolaya shakes his head. "They are victims, too. Humans are never taken willingly from their world. To leave them trapped in this false sleep is unthinkable."

"What if they are like Ell-ee?" Cashol says, and earns an angry glare from Bek. "Hear me out. What if they have been captive for so long they do not think like a human? What if they think more like those that arrived here to take captives? What do we do then?"

"The males look as if they would be dangerous, but we cannot free only the females," Pashov adds in. "That is cruel and unfair as well."

"There is no choice but one." Vektal's expression is firm. "Just because some of who have arrived here are enemies does not mean that all are enemies. Just because we have mates now does not mean that we cannot be kind to other newcomers who arrive here, stranded and taken from their homes."

We have mates. His words echo bitterly in my mind. I am the only one here who has no one waiting at home for him. The only one whose khui is utterly silent. I glance over at Brooke, and she's staring into the fire, her arms folded on her knees, her expression thoughtful. If she is pained by such words as I am, she does not show it.

"They are people," Vektal continues. "And they need our help. We will not abandon them. We will wake them and help them survive."

"What if they want to leave?" Ereven asks. "What if they wish to take the ship and return with it to the stars? And what if they lead others here?"

"We will never be safe," says Bek, furious at the thought.

Vektal puts up his hands, indicating silence. "I understand your fears. Georgie and I have thought long and hard about this, trying to consider every angle. We will rescue these people, but they cannot leave."

"How are we going to stop them?" Mardok asks. "If they know how to pilot a ship—"

"We are going to destroy the ship," Vektal says in a firm voice. "That way no one can use it against us. No one can use it, no one can leave with it, and no one will be able to trace it here. We will burn it from the inside out, and then we will dump it into the great salt lake."

Har-loh gasps.

Mardok is silent. He does not look pleased with this revelation, but when Farli reaches for his hand, he gives hers a squeeze. "It must be done," he agrees. "If we are to be safe, we need to get rid of anyone else's chance to leave. Anyone that goes back to the stars is sure to leave a trail behind them, and that trail leads back to us. Look at what happened to the old crew." He chokes up a little.

"But...we're going to let all of this go to waste? Think of what it could do for our people," Har-loh says. "Think of the lives we could save. Think of the benefits—"

"I think of all of that," Vektal tells her. "But then I think of the slavers. And I think perhaps we are safer without it."

She nods, slowly, though it is easy to see the hurt in her eyes.

"Mardok, Har-loh, can you make this cave fly?" Vektal focuses on them. "We can take it to the great salt lake, wake our new tribesmates there, and then let the sands slowly cover it with time."

"I can do you one better," Mardok says, and grips Farli's hand tightly in his own. "I can program the cursed thing to drive itself into the ocean for you, if you like."

Har-loh looks at him, wringing her hands. "We'll need a day or two to prepare, I think."

Vektal nods. "Then it is decided. You will have your two days, and then we ensure no one comes to our world again."

12

TAUSHEN

The mood is a somber one this evening. Everyone is anxious over what the future will bring, and Har-loh and Mardok have retreated back into the ship's belly, no doubt to discuss what they will be allowed to scavenge before Vektal orders it all destroyed. The fire is kept high, a ridiculous amount of fuel being spent to ensure the flames stay strong, but no one seems ready to go to bed and greet the next day. Instead, we gather and talk. Or rather, some talk, and I listen and watch.

I eye Brooke as she pulls her knees to her chest, hugging them close as she listens to Salukh talk proudly of his son, Lukti, and his efforts at tanning. Cashol and Zolaya are trading stories about their pregnant mates and the strange things they have been asked to bring them to eat. I envy them the pride in their voices, the eagerness for the future. They have many things to look forward to.

I have nothing more than the same. Every day, alone. My khui refusing all. I feel as if it holds me against my will, preventing me from happiness. Perhaps I should wish for the same fate as Haeden, to have my khui die in my breast so it can be replaced by a new one...but Haeden almost lost his life and sanity when that happened.

Perhaps it is better to be alone and miserable.

Brooke gets to her feet, faking a yawn. She murmurs something to Salukh, touching the arm of the tunic he is showing her, and gives him her broad I-want-things smile. I scowl in her direction, wondering what it is she says. What it is she asks him. But then, she leaves, faking a delicate yawn, and heads into the ship. Her yawn is as false as her smile, I realize. When she was with me that night, her yawns were huge and back-breaking. I had thought them charming in their ferociousness. It only adds to the strange puzzle that is Brooke. Why does she put on a face for others?

I wonder what she would think if I asked her about it.

I wonder if now is such a time. She is alone, I think, and that will not happen much in the future. I get to my feet.

Before I can go anywhere, Rokan and Hassen sit next to me. Hassen puts a hand on my shoulder. "Sit. We should talk."

"Talk," I echo, surprised. "What of?" I thump back to the ground, doing my best not to look after Brooke's retreating back as she heads up the ramp.

"You and Buh-brukh," Rokan says, voice calm and easy. "It is clear to us that something happened between the two of you. Was it when you were captive or after?"

I sputter, surprised that it is that obvious, and a little angry that even such a thing cannot be kept from tribesmates. I look to Hassen, but he has a brotherly grin on his face.

"Was it resonance?" Hassen asks. "You can share such things with us. We will know soon enough anyhow."

"If it was resonance, would Rokan not already know?" I snap. "He seems to know everything already. Ask him what I dreamed about last night."

"The enemy," Rokan says simply. "You have not slept well since they arrived."

I choke back my protest, because he is right. Shocked, I stare at him.

Rokan only shakes his head. "You dream of the same things any hunter would. It does not take my 'knowing' to realize such a thing. I do not think anyone has slept well since Bek and the others arrived back at the village with only half the group and a terrible story. We all worry over what will change."

"But we cannot fix such matters, so we will attempt to fix your problem," Hassen says, elbowing me and grinning. "Speak. So it is not resonance, then? You would not be so prickly if it was. You would be strutting about, waving your cock as if it is the most clever of creatures for spawning a kit in a female, just like those two do." He waves a hand at Cashol and Zolaya.

I snort. "You did the same when your Mah-dee resonated to you."

"I did," he agrees, good-naturedly. "I was so proud of my cock you would think it had dragged on the ground because of its size."

Rokan just chuckles. "Now there is an image I will have in my nightmares."

"We are a tribe," Hassen says. "We help each other out. We laugh together, we strut when we are proud, and we help when someone needs it. Are you sure you are not troubled, my friend?"

For a moment, I think to get up and snarl that I am fine. That I do not need his jokes about resonance and I do not want to hear stories of how happy he and his Mah-dee are. Once, I cast my gaze on the sisters, hoping to resonate, but my chest remained empty of song, and my furs have remained empty until now. Until Brooke, who never wanted my touch. The thought makes my gut ache, and I rub a hand on my forehead. "Have you ever wanted a female that did not want you back?"

"Yes," Hassen says simply. "They are called 'humans' and they love to tease a hunter before coming to his furs."

I just groan.

Rokan watches me, curious. "You and Buh-brukh, then. You care for her, but...she does not feel the same?"

It is difficult to explain, and I do not know if I want to share what happened between us with them. I do not wish for Brooke to feel uncomfortable around them at the realization that she came to my furs when she was not herself. She has said nothing to the others, and that tells me that it is a private matter, at least to this human. In a tribe as small as ours, everyone knows when plea-sure-matings occur, but perhaps Brooke does not feel the same.

Or perhaps she is ashamed of what happened. I hate that thought. "I cannot say."

Rokan only nods slowly. "But you are troubled, and it is about more than just whether or not you can woo her to your furs."

He is right. I glance over at him, wondering how much he can see with his "knowing." "Will she resonate to one of the new males? Will I resonate to one of the new females? These are my greatest worries. We are the only two unmated tribesmates here, and we will be adding twenty new people. I should be excited at the prospect, but instead, my heart is filled with dread."

"Because it is already given to another," Hassen says.

I nod. Again, he is right. I look to Rokan hopefully. Perhaps he can give us some guidance.

But Rokan only shakes his head. "I do not know these newcomers. Until I have spoken to them, I think my 'knowing' has nothing to see. They are as new snow to me. I can see no footprints of where the future will lead."

"And what of me?"

Rokan tilts his head. "Do you truly wish to know?"

Dread fills me. He knows something, then. Do I ask? Or do I wait for whatever the future will bring? But in the end, I must find out. "I do wish to know."

"I see resonance in Buh-brukh's future," he tells me simply. "More than that, I cannot say. But I feel it is close for her."

I am shocked—both at his words and at the wave of jealousy that sweeps through me. So my pink-maned, teasing Brooke is to belong to another male? I clench my fists. I want to pound them against something, but there is nothing nearby but the fire and my friends. My jaw tightens, and I flex my hands over and over again, tightening and loosening into fists. Bitter anger floods through me.

Brooke should be mine, but my khui is a coward, too afraid to claim a female. Because of this, I will lose her to another.

The thought fills me with despair. My hand clenches, this time over my heart. If I could reach in and rip my khui out, I would. "Then I am lost," I tell them, voice hoarse.

"Bah," Hassen says. "Take what you want. If you want Buh-brukh for yourself, claim her. Grab her and take her high into the mountains and bring her back when her belly is full of your kit."

"As you did my Li-lah?" Rokan asks, and his tone is deceptively mild. "How did that end up for you, my friend?"

"Very well," Hassen tells him, all smiles. "Because I saved her for you and mated her fierce sister who still attacks me as if I am to be conquered." He sighs, contentment etched into his broad face. "Mah-dee is a magnificent female."

"It turned out well because I rescued my Li-lah when she had run away from you," Rokan all but bristles, and I am surprised to see his reaction. Even after all this time, he still grows protective of his gentle mate. Of course he does. He adores her, as much as Hassen adores her much louder, more forthright sister.

"Do not snarl at me." Hassen leans forward, hands on his knees as he looks around me to Rokan. "I never tried to mate her, not once. She cried far too much."

Rokan bares his teeth. "Do not even put the thought in my mind, or I will rip your throat out. My Li-lah—"

I jump to my feet, slapping each of them on the shoulder with affection. "You have my thanks, friends. You have given me much to think about. I appreciate your advice." And I hurry away before the fight can become physical. They are good friends, Rokan and Hassen, but when it comes to one's mate, nothing else matters but her.

Nothing else matters but a mate.

Nothing else matters but her.

I ponder this as I head into the ship. I do not head for my own sleeping chamber, but the one where I know Brooke sleeps at night. The halls are eerily silent, and I place my feet on the strange stone floor carefully so as to not make a sound. I do not want to talk to her, just to check on her. To know that she is all right. That she is not troubled. That she sleeps well.

I hear a gentle humming as I approach. Quietly, I lean in and peer around the corner, into her open door. Brooke sits with her back to the entrance, her legs folded underneath her. She rests on the floor in a pile of furs, and as she hums to herself, she unbraids her hair. It is such a simple, achingly beautiful moment that my chest hurts just to watch her.

I want this. I want to be with her, at her side when she prepares for bed. I want to watch her hum as she unwinds her plaits every night.

Her humming wobbles, and then she yawns, her jaw cracking with the intensity of her yawn. Then she smacks her lips, and I am reminded of the night we spent together, and I ache with loneliness for her.

I move away, heading to my own sleeping furs. My mind is full of thoughts, and all of them center around Brooke. She will resonate to another, and soon...unless I do something about it, as Hassen says. Perhaps I should do as he did and steal away the female I intend for myself.

Do I not deserve happiness as much as these strangers?

The more I think about it, the more the idea has merit. I can take Brooke away, hide her from the others in one of the many hunter caves dotting the snowy mountains. There, I can woo her until she comes to my furs of her own accord. We can be happy together.

And if I must keep her away from the others forever, perhaps I will do just that.

I need a plan.

∼

I CONTEMPLATE how I will steal my female away. I think on it all morning and come to no conclusion as to how I will do such a thing. Brooke is smart, and she will be wary. If I throw her over my shoulder and take her from the camp by force, she will scream and she will hate me. If I snatch her from her furs while she sleeps, I will terrify her.

Nor will I even consider getting her drunk on sah-sah. That is out of the question. I want her to be fully aware of what is happening at all times so she will not feel like I am abusing her trust the way the slavers did.

So I will need trickery. I will not steal her away by force, not after what we have been through. I will need to somehow lure her away from the others...and then somehow convince her to stay. She will be angry, I think, but I will take her anger over losing her to another.

There is more to consider, though. My chief will be furious with me. If my choice is exile with Brooke or a life of loneliness surrounded by all my happily mated tribesmates, I will choose exile. That is not the problem. The problem is that I must somehow steal Brooke away without the others coming after her and taking her back.

I must let someone know my plans so they can reassure the chief that all is well...and take some of the heat off of me.

I decide to speak to Hassen and Rokan again. If they know my plans, they can reassure the others.

And they can lead them away from us, if needed.

13

BROOKE

*T*he vibe around camp is super weird.

I can't tell what it is, but we all seem to be tense. Well, no, that's not right. I know we're all tense because we're waiting to see what changes the pod people bring. Harlow and Mardok are stressed, but I think it's more about the ship than anything else.

And Taushen? Taushen just acts like he's too busy to talk to me. It's completely and utterly frustrating. I've tried to approach him to talk about that night, and to see if we can just be friends, but he's either rushing off to go hunting, or mending his weapons and talking near the fire with Rokan and Hassen.

It's almost like he's deliberately avoiding me. It shouldn't hurt my feelings, but it does. I kind of hoped we could at least be friends, but I guess that's too much to ask, after all. It pisses me off, mostly because I feel like things are spinning out of my control and I don't know how to fix it.

So I do what I can. I'm a hairdresser, so what I can provide that's useful is limited. I can't hunt. I don't know how to work the computers on the ship. I'm terrible at mending weapons and not great at cooking or watching the fire. There's always someone around that can do those things better than me, and every time I try to help out, I get a "Here, Buh-brukh, let me do that."

But I make sure Harlow, Farli, and Liz all look fierce with intricate braids. A woman that feels pretty is a powerful woman, after all. As I braid, I listen as Harlow complains about missing her son and worry over the new baby and her concerns over the ship we're going to destroy. She worries over Rukh, too. Poor Harlow's just got a lot on her plate. Liz is less complainy, but she wants to tell me all about her girls at home and how Aayla's a fierce little huntress like her mom, but Raashel prefers to learn in classes with Ariana and she wishes she had books for her to read. How she and Raahosh are ready for another kid, maybe a son this time, though she'd like another girl because hers are so fantastic. How she worries that the newcomers are going to overbalance things and upset our tiny ecosystem in the village. Farli worries over Mardok and how he'll take the destruction of the ship, and it's clear she cares for him intensely. She doesn't know how to help him with his grief over missing his friends and their terrible fate, and she worries she'll say the wrong thing and make it worse. I cluck and make appropriate sympathetic noises, letting her lead the conversation.

One of the things a hairdresser's good at? Listening. So I let them pour it all out on me while I braid, and in the end, I hope I've done my small part to ease their minds. Sometimes it's good to talk to another woman about your problems instead of your man. Your man is going to want to fix it. Another woman will listen sympathetically while you bitch and will take your side, no matter how wrong or crazy your side may be.

When I've finished with the ladies, I tie my own hair back into a pair of short braids, imagining how bad my roots must look at this point. I need some ice planet hair dye, stat. Well, maybe not "stat." I guess it's lower on the priority list than, say, food, shelter, and safety.

I weave cord near the fire as some of the others—including Taushen—head off to clear a nearby cache of its frozen meat. The newcomers are sure to be hungry, and Vektal wants to make sure there's enough for all. By the fire, Ereven is stirring a pouch full of greasy paste of what will eventually be trail rations. His messy hair flips down over his shoulder and falls forward for what feels like the dozenth time, and he flicks it back over and over. It bugs me enough that I get to my feet and move to his side, tapping his shoulder. "Want me to do your hair?"

"Do my hair?" He gives me a curious look. "What will you do to it?"

"Just braid it to keep it out of your way," I tell him, gesturing at his horns. "Probably do a gathered braid between those bad boys and then weave it in to a longer French braid. It'll be manly, I promise." When he hesitates, I put a hand on my hip and give him my most winning smile that's eased many a nervous customer. "Oh, come on. It's just a braid. If you hate it, you can take it out. And I've done lots of guy hair before."

He grins. "Very well, but if it looks ridiculous, you must remember so we can tell my Claire all about it."

I chuckle at that unexpected response. "I'll do you one better. If it looks completely silly, I'll recreate it when we get home so Claire can have a good laugh."

His face lights up at the thought of making his mate smile, sweetheart that he is, and I move behind his back, careful to watch his head movements so I don't get stabbed in the tit with a horn. Farli's done that to me a few times on accident and it wasn't pleasant. I drag my hand through his thick hair, finger-combing and feeling out the length. It's clear to me that Ereven cuts his own hair, because his ends are jagged like they've been sliced with a knife, and they're cut in all different lengths. Heavens. I would cringe if this came into my salon, but it's clear that Ereven isn't big into style. That's all right. Something simple, then, that gets the job done but won't take too long and isn't overly fussy. He's already twitching like a five-year-old getting his first haircut.

I separate a section of his hair and then begin to plait, weaving easily. The sa-khui hair is thick and coarse, almost like a horse's mane, but still manages to fall and style beautifully. I'm kind of envious of it. It's so much easier to style than my own flyaway hair that has to be cut just so or it looks raggedy. "Your hair is fantastic," I admit to Ereven as I tie off his braid. "All done."

"Eh?" He touches it and then swings his head from side to side. "Much better. Do I look foolish?"

"You look very handsome," I tease. "Claire would be proud."

"Can you do mine?" Zolaya asks, moving to examine Ereven's hair more closely.

"Like his?" I ask.

"No, do mine better." He grins at Ereven, who pretends to kick him.

I giggle, gesturing at the ground before me. "Have a seat and I can do your hair. *Better*." I tease. "So much better." I wink at Ereven to let him know that it won't be better, after all.

My skin prickles with...something. I glance over. Taushen's off to one side, his spear in hand, a backpack in the other. He's watching me as I run my fingers through Zolaya's hair, and Ereven says something silly. The look on his face is downright thunderous.

It's almost like he's...jealous.

Gah. I really do need to talk to him. I open my mouth to say something, but he turns and storms away, snow flying in every direction as he stomps.

Okay. I'll talk to him later, I decide. When he returns and he's worked off whatever pissy mood he's gotten himself into.

I DON'T SEE Taushen for the rest of the day. Everyone works feverishly all day, and I braid more cord than I've ever braided in my life, so much that my hands hurt by the time the suns go down. I've also braided the hair of most of the guys in the tribe, who appreciate my skills. Bek and Raahosh just give me strange looks when I ask them if they want their hair done, I'm too chicken to ask Vektal if he wants me to style him, and Taushen is nowhere to be found. I hang around the fire that night, even if I don't feel very social, and head off to bed, wondering. I hope he's okay. Maybe I shouldn't worry, but I can't help it.

Taushen's probably the person I'm closest to right now on this planet. Given the fact that he hates me, that's a sad statement if there ever was one.

When I wake up the next morning, though, the large group is scattered. The only one at the fire is Hassen, and he stands up when he sees me. "Good, you are here."

"I'm up, yeah." I'm also mystified as to why it's good that I'm here. Does someone need their hair braided? I mean, it's not like my skill set is vital to survival. Having fantastic hair isn't going to solve anyone's problems. I don't get why he looks so pleased to see me. I glance behind me, just in case he's not talking to me at all, but nope, I'm the only one here. "What's going on?"

"Vektal wants you to go to the fruit cave with one of the hunters and gather what you can for supplies."

Oh, the fruit cave? I guess I'm going to the damn thing after all, after avoiding it before. Still, fruit-picking will at least let me be useful instead of sitting around here with my thumb up my ass offering braids. And I'm pretty sure we have enough rope to tie up a hundred people at this point, so I've tapped out my usefulness. "Okay. Should I get my bag?" I hitch the fur wrap tighter around my shoulders, wondering if I need to layer, but the day is warm... for an ice planet.

"No, you will not be staying overnight." He gestures off in the distance. "He waits for you over that ridge."

He? "Who?"

But Hassen is already walking away, hefting a heavy basket of frozen dung chips—the fuel for most fires—under one arm and lugging it into the ship. Oh well. I guess I can find out. I bend down to lace my boots a little tighter and then slog through the snow in the direction Hassen pointed me.

I'm not entirely surprised to see Taushen waiting for me, a pack slung over his shoulder. I should have guessed that fate was going to stick us together. He scowls at the sight of me, looking me up and down, and just his pissy expression makes my back stiffen. He doesn't have to look so...annoyed at my presence. Like I chose to go with him? But I paste on a cheery smile and bound to his side. "Looks like you're my fruit-picking partner, huh?"

Taushen gives me a short nod.

"Well, let's try to have fun, okay?" I beam at him, but he only gives me a wary look. Wow. What's crawled up his butt?

"Come. Try to keep up." He turns his back to me and starts to stride away, forcing me to jog behind him to keep pace.

Oh, this is gonna be *fun*.

14

BROOKE

*I*t takes me a few hours to realize something's a little fishy about all of this.

First of all, Taushen's mood seems to improve the farther away we get from the ship. The angry set of his shoulders eases, his strides slow so I can keep up easily, and when I talk to him, he doesn't snap at me. Progress. It makes the walking not so bad, and we're able to have a few enjoyable conversations. I want to ask him about that night, get it all out in the open, but I also have to spend the entire day with the guy. I'll bring it up on the way back, when the day is over.

Until then, I just enjoy the day. The suns are shining, the snow isn't so slushy that it's a chore to walk, and I'm out in the wild. I'm not much of a wilderness girl at heart. I'm more of a mall girl, but I have to admit there's a strange, stark kind of beauty about this place. The snow is pristine and gorgeous, the distant mountains a stunning shade of purple capped with white, and the strange whippy pink trees flutter back and forth in the wind. When the bushes rustle with their frozen needle-like leaves, it almost sounds like music. I've never really had a chance to get out and explore much of this world, and it's fascinating to see it out in the open like this. The world from the view of the little village in the canyon's very different than up here in the sunlight and the open skies.

I kinda like it.

"Man, this walk sure is taking forever," I admit to him as we slog along. My boots are soaked from the snow, and my toes are cold. "How much farther to the fruit cave?"

He hesitates, then shrugs his big shoulders. "Not far. Do you need to rest?"

"No, I'm good." I rub my stomach. "I thought we'd be there before lunch, though. I'm starving. Feels like time's passing so slow."

"Hiking will make you hungry," he says, pulling a pouch from his belt and offering it to me. "Eat."

"Thanks," I tell him, and when I open the pouch, I'm not entirely surprised to see the meaty granola stuff of the travel rations. It starts out in cakes, but I guess the longer it gets jostled on a hip, the more crumbled it becomes. This one's just a big pile of crumbles, but I devour them anyhow. "You want some?"

He shakes his head, gaze on the horizon.

I chew happily as we walk. "So tell me a story while I eat," I beg him. "Talk to me."

Taushen glances over at me. "What kind of story?"

"Hmm. How about the biggest thing you've ever hunted?"

"That is easy. Sa-kohtsk."

Oh. Yeah, I guess that was a no-brainer. "Other than that?"

He thinks for a moment. "A sky-claw. Many seasons ago, they were very plentiful. I saw it in the skies and it was flying toward the direction of the cave, so I followed it and used my sling to throw rocks at it until it flew down to attack me." He gestures at a thin white line on his upper arm. "This is where its teeth grazed me."

My eyes widen. "How big are they? These sky-claw things?"

"Haeden says Jo-see was nearly swallowed whole once."

I sputter, choking on the trail rations. "There are birds that big *here*? Are you shitting me?"

He shakes his head. "I do not shit. They are very large. I do not know if they are birds or some other creature. They are dangerous, though."

I scan the skies, moving a little closer to him. "Do we have to worry about them?"

"Not this far inland. They like the great salt lake and the mountains. They rarely come in this far."

"But it *has* happened?"

"Yes, it has."

I swallow hard, suddenly a lot less hungry. "But you can kill them, right?"

The look he gives me is arch, smug. "I will keep you safe, Buhbrukh."

I elbow him. "You know my name, dickface."

"And you know mine. It is not dickface."

I sigh heavily. "Don't be a dickface and I won't call you one."

We trudge along in silence for a while. I tuck the pouch closed again and offer it back to him.

He takes it, his fingers grazing mine, and replaces it back in his belt. After a moment, he asks, "What is the largest kill you have ever done?"

Is he trying to get to know me? Extending an olive branch? Whatever it is, it's kind of sweet and I appreciate the gesture. "I think the biggest thing I've ever killed is a double meat bacon burger. I totally slaughtered that mofo. And now I'm wanting a burger."

"Was it fierce?" He glances over at me.

"It gave me fierce heartburn, but it was worth it. Also, you are hard to tease." I grin at him. "Mostly because you don't know what I'm talking about. Okay, so, a burger is a sandwich we have back on Earth. I guess you don't know what a sandwich is, either..." I gesture with my hands. "It's this round bread and you put things between it to make your meal. There are all kinds, and..."

We talk about food. I talk about the food we eat on Earth, and he is both amazed at how creative we are and a little grossed out at some of the things we eat, like eggs. I always forget that these people think eggs are nasty. He tells me about his favorite —fresh scythe-beak organs. Eww. From there, the conversation veers all over the place. I tell him about my home back in New Orleans, and how the floods from hurricanes can make a real mess of people's houses. I tell him about the swamps, the ocean, Mardi Gras, and how my granny's old house was haunted. I tell him about graveyard tours, and he thinks they are sad instead of morbid, and then we talk about how the sa-khui handle death, and how they mark up their horns and pour snow over their faces as they grieve, but nothing special is done with the body. It is left where it lies for nature to take care of. That's a little weird to me, but I roll with it.

Mostly, we're just having great conversation, and I'm learning so much about him and his people and getting to talk about myself and what I miss. It's hard to talk about Earth stuff with the other humans because you never know how they'll react. We're all from there, of course, but some miss it too much and avoid speaking about it. Some prefer not to think about it at all, and some just want to think about the future here, so we don't talk about it. But it matters to me, and it's good to get it all out in the open. It feels cathartic to talk about Earth, because the thought of never seeing home again doesn't ache quite so much anymore. Maybe I'm getting used to the thought of being here.

We're so lost in conversation that I don't even notice that my feet are cold until my entire body starts to shiver. I glance up, realizing that it's getting colder...and the now-cloudy skies are curiously dark. "Is it going to storm?"

"No. The suns are setting. Come, we are almost to shelter." He gestures at a hill in the distance. "Just beyond there, against the canyon wall."

"It's the fruit cave?"

"It is our destination," he agrees.

"Are we going to get in trouble that we got lost?" I ask him, weary. The day of walking is catching up to me. I'm hungry again, and exhausted. I can't believe time went by so fast. "I don't think the others expected us to take this long to get here. I didn't even bring an overnight bag."

"I will take care of your needs," he tells me simply, and then reaches out to pat my shoulder. "It is not much farther. Come."

I nod and follow him along, holding my fur wraps closer to my body. It's strange...I'm exhausted and I know we're probably going to get yelled at by the chief for getting lost and mucking things up and not making it back tonight, but I actually had a really nice day today. I've missed having long conversations with someone, and Taushen is surprisingly easy to talk to. I liked the scenery. I liked the company. Never thought I'd say that, but who knew.

And it feels important to tell him this, too. "I had a really nice time today," I say to Taushen as we crest the hill. "And I'm glad I came here with you."

He glances over at me, eyes narrowed, and searches my face as if looking for something. After a moment, a slow, almost hesitant smile crosses his face, making his sulky features inhumanly beautiful. "I am glad to be here with you, as well."

That reluctant, slow smile makes me realize just how little Taushen smiles. What a shame. He's really gorgeous when he does. It lights his whole face up, and I find myself smiling back at him.

A stiff wind rips through the valley we're walking in and I shiver. With the twin suns going down it's growing darker and colder—not that they exactly flood the place with light. My human body can't stand the chill.

Taushen pulls me against him, wrapping a warm arm around my shoulders as if he can lend me his body heat. "Almost there."

We make it to the walls of the valley, and I'm surprised to see the cave mouth is small and situated on the ground. For some reason, I thought Summer had mentioned climbing. Maybe she was talking about the journey here, I tell myself. It certainly was hilly enough.

Taushen puts a hand out, indicating I should stop. "Wait here."

"Is everything all right?" I ask, squinting at the cave opening.

He nods and strides forward, into the darkness of the cave. I wait outside as long minutes seem to tick past. Something that looks like a spark flutters inside, and then there's a bit of light. How strange, I realize. He's building a fire. Why do we need a fire if this is the ultra-warm, humid fruit cave, though? Does he think I need that to roast my dinner?

A moment later, Taushen jogs out and extends his hand to me. "Come inside. It is warm."

Mystified, I put my hand in his and follow him into the dark cave. As I do, I can't help but notice how warm and strong his callused hand is, how his fingers feel enveloping mine. I feel a wistful pang. Wish someone would hold my hand for me because they wanted to.

I'm so focused on hands that it takes me a moment to realize that there is, in fact, a fire.

And it's cold inside the cave. And dark.

And I don't see any fruit at all.

15

TAUSHEN

I see the expression on Brooke's face change when she realizes I have tricked her. I knew it was coming. I have been expecting this, and I am ready for her anger.

She gazes around the cave—a hunter cave, tucked away in the cliffs—and focuses on the rocky walls, the small interior, and then finally narrows her eyes at me. "You wanna explain?"

"This is not the fruit cave," I begin.

"No shit, Sherlock." She folds her arms over her chest and gives me a look.

I pause, because those words make no sense. When she does not explain, I continue on. "We did not get lost. I led you here deliberately."

Her fingers begin to drum on her arm. "Mmmhhmmm. Go on."

I shrug. "There is nothing else to say. Are you cold now that you are out of the wind? Should I make you tea?"

Brooke gapes at me. "No, I don't want tea. I want answers! Where are we?"

"In a hunter cave. There are dozens scattered in our hunting grounds." I move toward the fire, making sure that it continues to burn well. It looks to be a cold night, and I want to make sure my female stays warm. She needs the heat far more than I do. "When we are out on the trails for long times, we come to these caves to sleep and get supplies."

"Gee, that's nice. What are *we* doing here when we're supposed to be at a fruit cave, gathering food for the tribe?"

I stare into the fire for a moment, trying to think of the best way to phrase my answer. When no brilliant response comes to mind, I glance up at her. "I stole you."

"Stole me?" she repeats, emphasizing my words. "Why would you steal me?"

"It is a tradition amongst my people that when one wishes to mate a human, you steal her away to convince her." I feel exposed, vulnerable at such a confession. I do not want her to laugh or be offended. I do not want her to be angry that I have stolen her away from the others when she would have resonated to one of them. I do not mention that at all.

"You stole me because you want to mate me?" She smacks a hand against her forehead and groans. "Are you serious?"

"I am always serious," I tell her. Why does she need confirmation of such a thing?

"Taushen, buddy, we need to talk." Brooke bites her lip and tries to look patient, but fails. "You can't just freaking steal a person away. And you can't just mate me without my permission!"

"Then give me your permission."

"What? No! I'm not mating anyone!" She flings her hands into the air. "This is ridiculous. I can't believe you stole me! And I walked right into this!" She tilts her head back, staring up at the ceiling of the cave. "Incredible. I should have known that when it felt like ten hours of walking instead of two, it really was ten."

I say nothing. There are no words that feel right for this situation. I try to gauge her mood instead. Is she angry? Amused? It is difficult to tell.

She rubs her forehead and gives a deep sigh. "So what is this, then? You stole me because...?"

"Because you are mine," I tell her, surprised she has to ask such a thing. How does she not know this? Did I not tell her such things when we were together? "You belong to me."

That makes her angry. Her little brows go down and she scowls. "Slow your roll, buddy. I don't belong to anyone but me." She jabs a thumb at her teats. "Not to alien slavers, not to you, and not to anyone else that thinks they can put a collar on me and own me. Me."

Collar her? She thinks I would collar her?

I would never do such a thing. I want to take care of her and make sure all her needs are met. I want her to be happy. I want to hear her cries of pleasure and know that she is truly with me in both body and spirit. That when she clings to me, it is not because she has been given something to make her react in such a way. I want her to crave my touch as badly as I crave hers.

This is what I want. There are no collars involved, no strange drinks to make her react. There is only that which is freely given.

But the ability to tell her such a thing escapes me. I pause, trying to think of the right way to say how I feel. My throat tightens and I can only glare. "You...mine."

Brooke's delicate snort is derisive. "Thanks for asking how I feel about things before just deciding to run with your crazy ideas."

I did not ask her, this is true. But I knew she would not agree. She has never indicated that she would be willing to abandon the tribe for something as selfish as time alone together. And perhaps she wanted to stay behind because...because she wants to mate one of the newcomers.

The thought makes me burn with anger. Just imagining her in the arms of one of the strangers makes my resolve harden. I scowl up at her. "I did not ask, no."

"And so now we're here all night, alone. No one knows where we are. What if something happened to us?" She looks furious at me. I knew she would not be pleased that I lied, but...I do not know how to react in the face of her anger. Part of me thought she would be flattered at my declaration that I wished to mate her, not annoyed.

I have read the entire situation wrong. She hates me now.

"Nothing will happen to us," I tell her. Or try to, but she is not listening. She is pacing, her expression angry.

"All those hours of walking," she mutters to herself. "And I never even thought to ask why it was taking so long. I'm crazy."

I grunt. I have never thought of her as crazy. She is intelligent and clever, though I suspect she will not wish to hear that from me right now.

Her arms cross over her chest, emphasizing her magnificently protruding teats, and she whirls to face me again. "I'm an idiot for not asking, but you're a bigger idiot for thinking this was a good idea. They're going to the ocean tomorrow. The spaceship is leaving. My guess is that they'll just swing by to grab the two of us and then you're going to be in a shit-ton of trouble, Taushen."

Does she think I have not considered this? That I am a kit who thinks no further than his own hand? I straighten one of the rocks edging the fire pit, indignant. "They will not come for us. Hassen will tell them what we have done. They will assume we wish to be alone together."

"Hassen was in on this? That dirty little freak." She growls low in her throat, clenching her small fists with anger. "I am so telling his mate on him."

I almost grin at that, because I can just imagine boisterous Mahdee's response. She will probably yell at Hassen for a time...and then drag him to their furs so he can apologize to her properly. "As for Vektal..." I continue. "They will not be coming for us. They will respect our wishes to be alone and they will carry on their plan to take the others to the great salt lake. Hassen will tell them we will meet up with them there."

Brooke makes an outraged noise in her throat. "Respect *our* wishes to be alone, huh? Oh, for fuck's sake. You guys really have no concept of 'no means no.'" Her words are furious, but her expression is merely exasperated, as if I am a naughty, misbehaving kit. "Well, this was silly and a waste of a day." She gets her wrap and pulls it back around her shoulders. "We should get going if we're going to make it back."

"Make it back? We are not going back. It is late and you are tired." I gesture at the fire. "Come and sit here and warm up."

She looks at me like I am crazy. "We can't stay! They're going to think I want to be here with you."

That wounds me. Am I so terrible to be around? My pride makes me stiffen, and I gesture at the entrance of the cave. "I am not leaving. You are welcome to go."

A tiny part of me is curious if she will go. Farli would, but she is a huntress. Leezh would, because she is stubborn. And if she goes, I will follow, because I cannot bear the thought of her in danger, walking alone through the dark night. It is an angry dare, nothing more.

"Argh!" Brooke throws her hands up in the air. "I don't know how to get back!"

I have to stop myself from smiling. "Then it seems you will stay with me."

"You are such a creep for pulling this," she grumbles, flinging her wrap back off her shoulders and then sitting down on the floor near the fire and tugging at the laces of her sodden boots. "So now what happens?"

"You stay with me," I say simply, getting to my feet.

She looks up at me, disbelief on her face. "For how long?"

I have no answer for that. Until I no longer am burning with jealousy at the thought of her laughing at another male? Until the others have all resonated to different partners and I can bring her back? When she has no other option for a mate except me and my useless khui? Or until we tire of each other? Except I think I will never grow weary of her and her fierce spirit. I only seem to crave her more with each day that passes, until I am practically out of my head with the wanting of her. "Until you stop smiling at others," I say, deciding that is the best thing to tell her.

She makes another exasperated sound and throws her hands in the air. "You've got to be kidding. Smiling is a problem?"

"Smiling like you want something from them," I say, surly. "Like you think they are wonderful."

"You think I'm *flirting*?"

I shrug. We do not call it such in my tribe. It would be harmless if it were anyone else...but this is Brooke. My Brooke. I want all her smiles for myself.

"It's called being friendly, jackass. What have you got against that?" she asks, eying me curiously. Realization dawns on her face. "Are you *jealous*?"

There's a wondering note in her voice that makes my frustration rise. Does she not realize what she does to me? How her very presence makes me react? How much I want her?

"Of course I am jealous," I bite out, my tail flicking. "You smile at other males but never at me. You chatter and touch their hair, and ignore me. You touch their arms, but you hate my touch. You give your happy thoughts freely to others, and there are none for me. I want all of it. I want everything you have. I want your tears, your touches, your smiles, your frowns. I want it all, and I do not wish to share. I want to put you in my furs and devour you whole. The thought of four more males waking up and joining the tribe? Of you smiling and laughing with them? *Touching* them? Plaiting their hair? Taking them to your furs? It makes me crazy." I rake my hand through my mane in frustration, but it only falls over my horns and gets in my face.

"I think we're jumping to conclusions a little when you go from hair-braiding to sleeping together—"

"I do not want you resonating to them," I say fiercely. "I do not want any male near you. I want you as mine and only mine." My voice lowers to a growl as I meet her eyes. "Mine, Brooke. Mine and only mine."

"Resonate...to one of them?" Her voice is breathless and her gaze drops to my mouth, as if fascinated by my words. "I don't think so."

Rokan does, though. I keep this thought to myself. "You do not know for certain."

"I know I'm not ready to resonate to anyone," she says softly, stepping forward and closing the gap between us. Her gaze flicks over my face and then rests on my mouth again. "But I'm allowed to flirt if I want to. You don't own me, Taushen. You're not my father, either."

"I do not want to be your father," I snarl, beyond frustration. I am so full of need for her that I ache, and she speaks of her father? "I want to be your *mate*. The one who gets all your touches, all your caresses. The *only* one."

"That's so primitive of you," she breathes, and then she grabs me by my mane and pulls me down against her. Her mouth slams against mine, and then she's got her lips pressed to mine, and her tongue seeks entrance into my mouth.

I am stunned at her reaction—I thought she was furious with me. I thought she hated me.

But...her mouth on mine is fiercely sweet and insistent, and I cannot resist. I cup her face and return the kiss, pouring all my frustration and need into it. Let her see how much I need her, how much I crave her touch. My tongue slicks against hers and it is the best feeling in the world, second only to pushing deep into her wet, welcoming cunt.

Judging from the way she gasps in response, the soft noises she makes, I would wager she feels the same. That it is as good for her as it is for me. Her mouth breaks from mine and she sighs happily. After a moment, she moves her hand down my front and caresses my cock through my leathers with a throaty little chuckle. "Maybe you take your pants off and show me what you've got, hmm?"

Again, I am surprised by her response. To think she would be so passionate after telling me she did not want my touch...

Suspicion rises in my mind, and I think of the teasing smiles she has given other men. The laugh when she wants something. I was not paying attention, too distracted by her kiss to remember if the laugh she gave me was a true one or a fake one. "Do you do this because you want me?" I ask, breathing hard under her arousing touch. "Or because you wish for me to do something for you?"

She gasps and pulls her hand away as if burned, and I know in that moment I have made a mistake. "Maybe I just wanted to touch you, you dick." Brooke looks hurt, and I ache inside at her wounded expression.

I reach for her. "Then touch me."

"No!" she cries, snatching her hands away from me. "The moment's passed. You killed it dead." She pushes me away and takes a step back. "Way to go. Here I'd been feeling lonely and hoping we could..." She shakes her head. "You know what? You're an asshole, and I hope you're happy with having a super-bitchy companion for the next while because that's all you're going to get from me."

Panic rises inside my mind. She touched me because she wanted me? Not because she wished for me to do something for her? She wanted to mate and I have pushed her away?

This is my fault for not trusting myself. For not imagining that such a perfect female would truly wish for me. Not after what we have been through. "Brooke...I am sorry."

"It's too late for sorry." She rubs her arms, looking small and lost and hurt. I did this, and the realization makes my gut churn. She steps away. "Don't talk to me."

"I have made a mistake," I tell her. "I admit this. I did not think..."

"You thought I was going to flip my hair and suck your dick to get what I wanted? What does that say of your opinion of me?" Her look is scathing, and I realize with shame that she is right.

I have acted terribly. I have pushed her away, and this time it is no one's fault but my own.

16

BROOKE

*B*y the time morning comes, I'm no longer angry. I've had time to stew over the situation all night, and I've come to the conclusion that while deceiving me into a quasi-abduction was kind of headstrong and uncool...it was also really flattering.

No one's ever wanted me that much. All of my ex-boyfriends never seemed to give a crap when I broke up with them, as if I was totally disposable. My relationship with my family wasn't great, and all of my friendships seemed to fizzle out after high school as they all went on to go to college and I decided to do hair. Oh, they'd still call me when they needed drinking buddies for Mardi Gras, but it's not the same. Even now, the other human girls seem to be closer to each other than to me. It didn't really bother me too much, because at heart, I'm independent and like to do my own thing.

But...it's really nice to be wanted.

More than that, it's nice to be wanted so badly by someone that they're willing to risk their neck for me.

Granted, if I were back on Earth and Taushen was a one-night stand that wouldn't leave me alone? I'd be calling the cops. Things are different here, though, and sa-khui don't think like humans. I can't think like an Earth person when it comes to Taushen. Everything's different. I come from a culture where women are everywhere and it's just assumed you'll eventually settle down with the right guy and get married and produce a few kids. That you and your husband will get a nice little office job and then spend your weekends shuttling the kids to soccer practice and keeping up with the laundry. That food comes from a grocery store and the toughest decision you make about it is whether you want Honey Nut Cheerios or the plain ones.

Taushen's world is different. If you want to eat, you have to catch your food, kill it, and store it. You have to portion and prepare for the long winter—the brutal season. You can't have lazy days in bed and do nothing. And he grew up in a tribe that only had four women for almost forty men. More humans have come, but he still hasn't resonated, and there haven't been any single women left to play the field. The more I think about it, the more I'm almost positive he was a virgin when we got together.

In short, Taushen has no clue how to handle a relationship. Me? I'm used to the games. I'm used to feigning disinterest and not calling guys back for days—or weeks—to make it seem like I'm not all that interested. I'm used to playing the field. Most of all, I'm used to not needing anyone but myself. If a guy doesn't like me? Oh well, there's more fish in the sea. But poor Taushen doesn't have the same option. No wonder he feels desperate when he looks at me. I'm the only single girl. Well, up until tomorrow, I'm the only single girl, since I'm pretty sure Summer is now hooking up with Warrek. Tomorrow sixteen more women get woken up, though. Maybe if we hadn't had sex, Taushen would have transferred his affection onto one of them.

Problem is, we did have sex. I don't know how to detangle the knot we find ourselves in, either.

I like Taushen. I like him a lot. He's got a sweet core, and underneath that scowly exterior is a heart of gold. He's caring. It's obvious in how many times he woke up last night to stoke the fire and how he made sure I had enough furs to sleep comfortably, even if I wasn't talking to him. How he hung my boots so they'd dry properly and checked on them regularly throughout the night, turning them so they wouldn't sear. How he woke up super early this morning to refuel the fire, brew tea, and brought back fresh meat that he's roasting even now.

If he was a dick, he wouldn't bother. I've dated a lot of dicks in my life. I can spot them from a mile away. Taushen's like...an anti-dick. Maybe that's why I have such a hard time figuring out how to act around him. If he was one of those "Hey baby, I'll call you later" types, I'd know what mental category to place him in and wouldn't think twice. He's not like that, though. He just watches me from afar with his heart in his eyes, and it's clear he's anguished that I'm upset.

And even though I want to stay mad...I can't. I can't stay mad, but at the same time, I can't entirely forget everything we've been through. From the night we were imprisoned together to the fun conversations we had yesterday as we walked, I like Taushen too much to cut him off and be enemies.

It's a little problematic how much he likes me, though. He doesn't want me to resonate to anyone else. He thinks of me as his mate. I know some of that is his naiveté, and some of it is the fact that there haven't been other single women around for him to focus on.

And okay, some of it is because I'm sending him totally mixed signals. We had sex that I was totally into, only for me to tell him that, surprise, I wasn't into it after all. That has to be confusing for a guy who's never had sex and probably has never even heard of the concept of Spanish fly. To make matters worse, all of the things he was telling me last night about how much he wanted me?

I have to admit, it turned me on. I immediately responded with my natural instinct—to take things to the next step. I would have gone down on my knees and taken him in my mouth...except that he thought I was using him to get something. That hurt my feelings. It made me feel like, well, a whore. Like I was doing something wrong.

We've got to come to an understanding, though. I meant what I said when I claimed I didn't want to be anyone's mate. I still don't. I want to figure out who I'm supposed to be on this new planet before I go hitching my wagon to someone else. I want to be my own person. After bad relationships back on Earth and family that didn't give two craps about me unless they could use me, I went right to the slave pens and became someone's property. Then I arrived here, the planet of cooties and resonance, and while I'm lucky that hasn't hit me yet, I have a feeling that bullet's headed in my direction at some point. Until then, I want to enjoy just being...me.

Also, Taushen doesn't seem to grasp the concept of a casual hook-up.

So, yeah. We can't let things continue with the both of us angry at each other and frustrated. That doesn't work for anyone. It's a small tribe, and we need to learn how to get along. We need to come to an understanding for his sanity and mine.

I sit up in the furs, rubbing my eyes. I didn't sleep all that well, despite the cave being kept cozy and warm. I kept thinking about the situation I'm in. The situation we're both in, really. He's put his neck on the line to "claim" me as his mate, and I know that Vektal won't be happy with this, given how he reacted when Bek told them he was the one that brought us here. He's risked every-thing...for me. I mean, heck. He could be resonating to one of the new chicks, even now. The odds are better that he'll find a girl-friend out of sixteen than me finding a mate out of four new guys.

Funny how that thought doesn't sit so well with me. Maybe I'm all mixed up over the situation, too. The fact that we had really great sex—drugged or not—can't be helping things.

So I sit up and wait for Taushen to notice that I'm awake. When he does, I offer him a smile.

He looks surprised to see my reaction, and his own smile gradu-ally eases over his handsome face, and breaks my heart. Poor guy. He's so darn lonely.

"Can we start over?" I ask him, keeping the smile on my face to gentle my words.

"Start over?" he echoes, clearly not understanding what I mean. Instead, he practically scrambles to the fire, grabbing one of the hollowed-out bone cups and filling it. "Let me get you tea. Are you hungry? I have charred flesh for you for breakfast."

Yum, yum. Just hearing it said like that makes me lose my appetite, but I know he "charred" it for me. It's just another sign that he's trying really hard. I take the tea he offers me and try again. "When Earth people acknowledge they've screwed up, sometimes they try to start over. You know, start fresh." I give him my most winning smile. "Hi, my name is Brooke, and I'm a Scor-pio. I'm currently visiting other lands to find myself, and I like hot food, warm blankets, and long walks in the snow." I stick my hand out for him to shake. "You?"

He takes my hand gingerly in his own, examining it as if waiting for me to do something. "I what?"

"You introduce yourself," I tell him.

"But you know who I am." Taushen narrows his eyes at me, not following. "Did you hit your head somehow? Like when Pashov lost his memories?"

"This is us starting over. Like we're just meeting each other for the first time." I withdraw my hand from his, because he's touching it far too familiarly for just a simple handshake. "We've got too much baggage between us, you and I. It's interfering with how we are acting. It'd be better if we just started fresh, don't you think?"

"Start fresh." He says the words slowly, as if tasting them, and then his gaze meets mine. "So...you wish to pretend we have never met before?"

"Something like that, sure. We act like the past didn't happen, so we can start a new future together with fresh minds."

His jaw clenches stubbornly, and he shakes his head. "I do not wish to do this."

Exasperated, I sigh. "Why not?" Why is he making this so difficult? Is he determined to piss me off?

"Because I do not wish to forget what happened between us." The look on his face is earnest. "I know it was a terrible night for you, but it was the best night of my life. I will never forget it."

And just like that, all of my irritation fades away. "Oh, Taushen." I pat the blankets next to me. "Sit and let's talk, okay?"

He eases his big body down onto the furs next to me, and if he's sitting a lot closer than he probably should, I don't point it out. I clasp my hands in my lap, trying to think of the best way to broach the subject. "I really want to be friends with you," I tell him gently. "But I'm not sure we're on the same page."

"Friends?" Taushen frowns down at me. "I wish to be mates."

"Yep, that's the problem I've got. I'm not ready to be anyone's mate."

"If it were resonance, you would not have a choice," he says stubbornly.

"Which means I'm really glad it's not." I shake my head at him, frowning. "Why are you so fixated on resonance? Is it because it hasn't happened for you yet? You're young. It'll happen. You just have to give it time..."

As I speak, his face grows more and more shuttered, his expression tight.

I pause, studying him. "What is it?"

"It does not matter how much time I have," Taushen says flatly. "Resonance will not happen for me."

"That's not true," I protest, aching for him. It's clear that he wants this badly. "You don't know that. No one can predict the future."

"Rokan can."

Okay, he's got me there. "You know what I mean. Stuff can always happen." I reach out and take his hand in mine, squeezing it. "It'll happen for you. I promise."

The look on his face flashes to one of agony. "You do not know what you speak of."

Don't I? Is there something about the khui that I'm not understanding? "What do you mean?"

"I have never been chosen. Never."

The vehement way he says it makes me think there's a little more under the surface, an old festering wound. Is this what's made him so bitter? I remember Harlow's comment about him being so puppyish and eager once upon a time. "Tell me what happened."

"Nothing," he says angrily. "That is what has happened. "When human females arrived on our world, I thought, finally, I would have a chance. That I could have a mate and a family and all of the things I have longed for. The things I have dreamed of. Others resonated and I did not. I thought that was all right. That there was time and I would resonate to one of the females. I had one that I liked more than the others, too. Her name was Ti-fa-ni and she was beautiful. And I fought the others for her attention, only for her to resonate to Salukh."

"And it broke your heart."

"It hurt more that I was not chosen. Ti-fa-ni is a fine female, and Salukh is a good mate for her." He shakes his head. "I thought perhaps my khui waited for another. But then Jo-see resonated, and then there were no more females. There were so many in my tribe without mates that I did not feel abandoned. There were many hunters who ached for a mate, and the hunters' cave was full. But then Li-lah and her sister arrived, and I once again hoped." He shakes his head.

I know Lila. She's mated to Rokan. And Maddie's mated to Hassen. Both quite happily. "So you were passed over again."

Taushen's gaze is distant. "I thought perhaps I would wait for Farli, but as she grew older, I suspected my khui would never see her as a mate. She is too much as a sister to me."

"And then we arrived and you still didn't resonate to anyone."

His mouth thins. "I thought it would not matter so much if I had a pleasure-mate...but..."

But he slept with me, and then I made him feel guilty because I was under the influence. Yeah, it's kind of a mess. "I'm sorry, Taushen. There will be other opportunities. Sixteen new—"

"How many females must be paraded before my khui for it to finally notice one?" he explodes. "For it to deem me worthy of a mate?" When I open my mouth to speak, he shakes his head. "And do not tell me I can wait for one of the kits to grow up. I have had others tell me that." Taushen snorts. "As if every day is not lonely enough as it is, now they tell me to be patient and to wait twenty seasons."

"I wasn't going to say that," I tell him softly. "I just hate that you're hurting so much. I know what it's like to want something you can't have." Like...Earth. Home.

His gaze fixes on me. "It does not matter anyhow, the only one I want is you. Resonance or not, you are my mate."

And this is where it gets awkward. "Oh, Taushen. You—"

"You do not wish for me to be your mate. I know. But you wonder why I am so angry? So bitter? So frustrated?" He spreads his arms as if to say "see." "It is because my khui rejects all. It rejects any happiness I might have and remains silent. Forever."

I don't want to tell him that it's just waiting for the right girl to come along. I know how it feels to be told shit like that. So I put my hand on his knee in (what I hope is) a friendly gesture. "You're looking at this all wrong. Men on Earth would love to be in your shoes."

He scowls at me. "Explain."

"You're a single male, and there's gonna be a ton of single ladies in the tribe all of a sudden. You're one of a handful, and you're strong, brave, and smart. Girls are going to be falling all over you, looking for a protector."

"But you—"

I push ahead, because I don't want him declaring love for me. I don't know how to handle that. "Without resonance, you have freedom. Didn't Vektal play the field a little before he hooked up with Georgie?"

"Play in fields...?"

"Sleep around."

"Ah." He looks unhappy at the thought. "He and Maylak were pleasure-mates for a time, but she resonated to Kashrem a few seasons before he met Shorshie."

Again, more resonance talk. I shake my head. "You want freedom. It's the most important thing in the world."

Taushen meets my gaze, his heart in his glowing, sad eyes. "And is that what you want?"

I feel like my answer might break him, but at the same time, I don't want to lie. "After everything I've been through? Being enslaved and almost enslaved a second time? Dropped on this planet without being asked where I'd want to go? There's nothing more appealing than being able to choose my own fate for once."

He nods slowly. "And I have stolen your freedom from you again, have I not?"

"You didn't mean to—"

"I meant to," he admits, a grin crossing his face. "Be assured of that."

I laugh, because he's right. "Okay, you meant to. I'm just telling you what I thought you wanted to hear. It's called being nice."

"I do not want your nice. I want your honest."

I smile. "And I want your friendship. Nothing more for now. Can we just go with that? Just be friends without being weird about things?"

Taushen meets my gaze, but the strange tension on his face seems to have eased. "You do not hate me for stealing you?"

"Nope." I could never hate him. It's kind of weird, but I think I understand him better than anyone else on this planet. "I could never hate you."

He gives me a long, long look, and it's hard to tell what he's thinking. Eventually, though, he smiles once more. "Then I shall let you lead from this point onward."

"What do you mean?"

"If you wish for freedom, I shall give it to you." He makes a gesture at the cave, and sweeps his arm outward toward the front, where I can see the snowy ground outside. "Where would you like to go? Do you wish to return to the ship? To the tribe? The Elders' Cave? You choose. I am giving you freedom."

He is? I'm so astonished that I can't answer for a moment. "You're...letting me pick where we go?"

Taushen nods. "I shall take you wherever you like. You decide."

I blink and then pull my knees up to my chest, considering. At first thought, I want to say "I can't possibly pick," but that's because I'm used to letting others get their way. If I want freedom and to do things on my own terms, I need to learn to make my own decisions. So I think. Do I want to go back to the little stone city in the canyon? I'm not in any particular hurry, honestly. There's no one waiting for me back there. Go back to the tribe and meet up with Vektal and the others at the ocean? While I'm curious about the newcomers, I'm also not in a big rush to head in that direction, either. I do want to see the ocean...but not if it means I'm going to resonate to someone like Taushen's afraid of.

A thought crosses my mind, and I glance over at my companion. "I don't suppose we can go on vacation?"

Taushen pauses, a curious expression on his alien features. "Vacation? What is this?"

Now that I've said it aloud, I like the idea more and more. "A vacation. It's where humans decide they need a break from everyday life so they escape for a little while. They go traveling. Exploring. Do new things, just to change stuff up in their lives, and then they go back home again, refreshed and ready to take on their problems once more. We could do that. Have a little adventure of our own and see the world."

"You...do not want to rejoin the tribe right away?"

"No. Not if we could just do our own thing. Is it safe if we go traveling, just you and me? We're not going to get caught in a blizzard or anything, are we?"

He considers. "As long as we do not stay away for many moons. If we are back to the tribe before the brutal season, it will be fine." Taushen says the words slowly, as if he doesn't want to admit it. "They will need me as a hunter, though, especially if there are more mouths to feed."

"Then we'll hunt as we go," I tell him quickly. "You guys store food in caches, right? We can fill them as we go. It'll be vacation and work all rolled into one."

"But where would we go?" Taushen asks, a genuinely curious look on his face. It's as if he's never considered such a thing before.

"Anywhere we want to." I'm excited at the prospect. I remember car trips with my friends back after I graduated from high school, when we'd fill up the tank and just drive and see where it led us. I turn toward him on the blankets, eager to plan things out. "Do you ever just explore out on your own? What's your favorite place?"

He thinks for a moment, and then touches his horns. I'm curious about that, and then he begins to speak. "There is a cave...in the mountains a very long walk from here. It is close to where Shorshie and the others landed when they arrived. It is small, and the icicles that hang from the ceiling scrape your horns when you walk in. But...it is the most beautiful place I have ever been. Everything shines, and there is a hot spring that bubbles from the cracks in the rocks and it trickles down over a pond that has fish with no eyes." He closes his own eyes as if to demonstrate, and then opens them again. "They are pale and ugly, but they are good eating."

I clasp my hands, excited. "That sounds lovely. Let's go there!"

The look he gives me is uncertain. "It is a long walk."

"I don't mind walking. You can teach me how to hunt and follow tracks."

A half-smile tugs at his mouth. "Any kit can follow tracks. They are obvious in the snow."

I swat at his arm, chuckling. "Well, then give me the basics on how to handle myself in the wild, all right? You can teach me how to survive."

"This is what you wish to do?"

I nod, eager. "I think a vacation is just what the both of us need."

He rubs his chin, thinking, and then shrugs. "We can leave by midday then. If we pace ourselves strongly, we can make it there in a few days."

Midday? Today? I glance outside, where the snow is starting to fall thick on the ground. "This is vacation, dude. We don't have to be anywhere fast." I lean over and slouch down on the furs, relaxing. "We can just hang out."

"Hang...out?" He looks over at the propped spear, where my clothes are hung and drying.

"Not hang like that," I say, poking him in the leg. "Hang out like just relax. Enjoy the day. Be lazy. Crawl under the furs."

His eyes gleam. "Your furs?"

"Nice try."

17

BROOKE

*I*t takes Taushen a little time to warm up to the concept of vacation. It's almost like if he's not busy for every minute of every hour of every day, some invisible force is going to appear and slap his hand, chastising him. The first day of our official "vacation," we stay in the cave, hanging out and getting comfortable around each other again. We play games to make the time pass, and I rack my brain to try to come up with entertainment. Playing cards is out, since we don't have paper. I could probably manage to make bone dominos, except I don't know how to play anything like that. We settle into the most basic of games after a time—Truth or Dare and I Spy. I keep things squeaky clean because the last thing we both need is to muddy the waters between us with some filthy "dares." It's like it never occurs to him that the game can be played any way other than innocently. Taushen enjoys the heck out of the games, and nothing makes me feel better than seeing a genuine smile curve his hard mouth. He needs more smiles, I think.

It snows hard for two days, so we stay in our little cave. Well, mostly. Taushen makes me go out with him to the nearest cache, and we dig it up, counting inventory to make sure that the tally marks on the marker are correct. We excavate a frozen quill-beast, recover things, and then set a few traps so we can replenish before we leave.

Taushen catches sight of my wrinkled nose and distaste at the frozen dead animal and just hoots with laughter. "You said you wished to learn to hunt. I am teaching you."

"I would have said anything if it meant a vacation," I grumble, but I resolve to suck it up. Preparing what looks like frozen roadkill can't be worse than whatever they do to food at the chicken nugget factory back at home.

On day three, the weather clears, and we decide to head to the fruit cave to get a change in our diet. Plus, after a few days of snow, I'm looking forward to hanging out in a sauna-like cave.

At the fruit cave, we give ourselves a day or two to bake in the heat, eat all the fruit we can stomach, and then we head out back into the snows again, this time heading for Taushen's icicle cave in the mountains. We take our time walking, and as we trudge through the valleys and over rocky cliffs, we chat. Taushen's so easy to talk to, and our conversations are endless. It's like I can start on one topic and end up on a completely different one and he follows me completely. After a while, it's almost like our brains are in synch. We share stories of our childhoods, I tell him all about my horrible ex-boyfriends, and he offers to beat them up if they ever show up as slaves.

It's awesome.

The travel with Taushen actually makes me realize how long it's been since I had a true, honest-to-goodness best friend to share my thoughts and secrets with. I love it. I love that I can tell him anything and he won't judge me or think I'm silly. He thinks that being a hair stylist is wonderful, because I got to make people smile and feel good about themselves. He thinks that I'm smart and that I work hard. And even though he teases me about my hunting skills, I don't give up. Everyone's bad at everything in the beginning, and you just have to stick with things. I'm determined to stick with hunting, if nothing else, so he can be proud of me.

Every day we grow closer in our friendship, and I think I'm so lucky that we could be friends after everything that happened. That he's not trying to hold a grudge or possess me. That he's fine with being just friends.

It takes about two weeks before I start to wonder if I've made a mistake.

Maybe it starts when we get to the ice cave. After days on end of walking, hunting and traveling, we make it to our destination. On the outside, it doesn't look like much. As Taushen mentioned, the exterior of the cave is tiny, with the entrance so small that you have to bend over just to get inside. I can well imagine horns scraping along the rock, and I think he's brave for ever coming in here in the first place.

But then we get inside, and Taushen lights a torch.

And it's the most beautiful, surreal place I've ever been. Crystals cover every inch of the cave, as far as the eye can see. He's right that the ceiling isn't tall, and it's a bit like standing inside of a hollow egg. If I reach a hand up, I can touch the ceiling, and it extends, cocoon-like, into the rounded cavern. It's definitely too small to make a comfortable sort of cave.

But oh, the view. Thick, blocky crystals crust the ceiling. Long, drippy crystalline icicles hang along the edges and down the walls. Along the floor, stalagmites rise up to meet their sister stalactites, and those seem to be made of a shiny crystal as well. It's like stepping into a rock candy paradise...or a big people-sized geode. The torch that Taushen holds up seems to make everything glitter, and in the back of the place I can see the hint of the pond he mentioned, and the steam curls that let up from the water itself.

It's incredible, and I tell him that. I'm surprised he's not looking at it, but his gaze is fixed on me, as if he doesn't want to miss a moment of my reaction.

"I come here when my heart is sad," Taushen says softly. "And somehow, this place makes my spirit glad once more. That I can see such a place and touch it. That I can live where such a thing can exist, and then, perhaps, I think everything is not so bad."

And my heart just aches and aches for him.

I just wanted to be friends...didn't I? Just wanted my freedom.

Wasn't interested in a partner. At all.

Guess I'm pretty good at lying to myself, because what I'm feeling right now is decidedly...un-friendlike.

That could be a problem.

Ever since we've decided that we're going to be friends and just friends? Things between us have been so, so great. I haven't felt uncomfortable around him and there hasn't been any weird tension. We can laugh together about the dorkiest of things, and even when there's accidental nudity or something equally embarrassing, we both just laugh it off. The friendship is the only thing that matters, and now it's like all the anxiety is gone and the only thing left is the awesome, easygoing vibe between us. It feels like a deeper, unshakable bond than just sex.

I'm scared to mess it up.

I'm also ashamed to admit to myself that I've been thinking about the sex a lot.

Maybe I'm a perv at heart. Maybe I can't have a friendship with a guy without wanting to get him in the sack. Maybe I'm the problem, but it seems like the closer we get as friends and the more I know about Taushen, the more I wonder if I've made a mistake.

Perhaps I shouldn't have been so quick to scream freedom and I should have let the guy claim me instead. Of course, then I'd have to give up our wonderful friendship, which right now is the only good thing about this ice planet.

That and this gorgeous cave, of course.

I can't change the vibe between us, though. Things have been going so good.

I tell myself that we can just be friends. That sex doesn't matter.

That I shouldn't notice the way his arms flex when he throws his spear. Or the way his face lights up when he sees me wake up in the morning. Or the delighted laugh he gave when I flung a snowball down the back of his tunic and then tried to run (unsuccessfully) for the hills before he caught me.

I shouldn't notice that his tail is incredibly mobile and it moves with his mood. If he's sleepy, it flicks slowly. Angry? It lashes. Pleased? It's a sensuous undulation that moves back and forth and makes me think dirty, dirty thoughts.

I also shouldn't notice that I like the way he smells when he sweats, or that he makes the most adorably sexy groans when he sleeps, as if he's dreaming about dirty, sexy things.

My mind is definitely in the gutter lately, and that's a problem.

I'm the one who demanded friendship. I feel like I can't change my mind now, even if I wanted to.

I wanted freedom, and I got it. I wanted a friend, and I got it.

Didn't think I'd want more than that.

18

TAUSHEN

"*T*hat was so beautiful," Brooke tells me dreamily as we lie beside the fire that night. "Thank you for taking me there."

She reclines across from me, stretched out on her pallet of furs in the hunter cave we have bunked down in for the night. The fire flickers between us, and she props her head on one arm, gazing into the fire. I sit across from her, legs crossed as I tend the fire and warm tea for us. After weeks of traveling, I know how Brooke likes her tea, and I make it without being asked now. It is a small thing, but I like pleasing her.

I nod. "It is my favorite place." And it feels good to share it with her. It feels right, like I have exposed a part of my spirit and shared it with her. I like that thought. "I am glad you liked it."

Her smile is sweet but distant, and she continues to gaze into the fire thoughtfully. She has been quiet this day, and when I asked her about it, she only said that she was thinking about the cave. I worry something is wrong, but I do not know how to ease into the subject. I have learned much about my Brooke over these last days and nights, and I know that she will talk about things, but in her own time. She does not like to be rushed. So I decide to care for her in the only way I can, at the moment. I offer her a pouch of travel rations, and when she declines it, ask, "Tea?"

She shakes her head.

"Not thirsty?"

"Just thinking." Her gaze meets mine and she smiles softly. "Weirdly enough, thinking about the others and the twenty newcomers. I wonder how they're doing with them."

I ignore the stab of jealousy in my stomach. We are friends, I chant mentally. Nothing more than friends. If this is all that I can have of her, I will take it and be glad. I tell myself such things a dozen times a day in the hopes that one day I shall believe it. So far, though, it is not working. I still dream of Brooke and her soft limbs every night, and when I wake, it takes every bit of my strength to not cross the small cave and pull her into my arms. To kiss her until she decides she wants me as much as I want her.

Being "friends" has not eased the ache for her. It has only made it worse.

"Thanks for traveling with me," she says, the thoughtful note still in her voice. "Feels like I'm getting to see stuff I'd never get to see otherwise."

"Eh? Why would you not get to see such things?"

She shrugs. "Seems like most of the girls don't travel much. They either have kids or are pregnant, so I guess that puts a damper on the wandering spirits."

"Leezh and Mah-dee have kits," I point out. "And Li-lah. They enjoy traveling with their mates."

"Yeah, because they have a mate with them. I'm single, remember? No one to watch my back."

I would watch it for her. "I will go to the ends of the land if you wish to. Anywhere you want to go, we will go."

Her smile curves her mouth, and then she gives a soft chuckle. Her sweet, happy, true chuckle that makes my chest ache with want. "What if you resonate?"

"She can wait."

Brooke just laughs even harder, shaking her head. "Says a man that hasn't resonated. I suspect it'd be different if your ladylove was waiting for you." She gives me a thoughtful look. "You think it'll happen this time?"

"No." I hope she does not ask me if I think it will happen for her. I worry my face will give away the truth.

"Mm. If you could pick a mate, any mate, would you pick a sa-khui or a human?"

"There is no sa-khui female of appropriate age to mate."

"I know. We're playing a game of pretend." She gives me an exasperated look. "Go along with it."

A game? It sounds like a dangerous one. I give her a wary look. "Very well. I would pick human." My mind cannot wrap around the thought of picking another female. There is only Brooke in my mind.

"Dark-skinned or light-skinned?"

I sense a trap. Does she wish for me to confess my feelings for her again? To tell her that they have never changed? That I wake up every morning with no desire but to see her smile? That I care for her more and more every day? That the thought of bringing her back to the tribe and watching her resonate to another fills me with dread? But if I tell her such things...will it ruin our friendship we have built? Will she get uncomfortable around me and will our easy camaraderie disappear? I worry it will be so, and so I choose the answer least like her. "Dark."

She nods, as if considering this thoughtfully. "Dark hair or light hair?"

Pink, I think to myself. "Dark."

Her brows draw together, and she gives me a curious look. "So... basically like Tiffany."

I shrug. What is the answer she wishes to hear? That I dream of the pink waves of her mane tickling my stomach as she curls up against me in her sleep? That I wish I had never stopped her when she put her hand on my cock? That I want her to demand more from me than just companionship?

I do not want to lose what we have, though. So I say nothing.

BROOKE

His perfect woman is Tiffany.

Damn it, I fucking hate Tiffany. I don't even know her all that well, and I hate her. I hate her pretty face and her bouncy curls and her smile and how she's good at everything. Oh, you want leathers? Talk to Tiffany, she's the best at dyeing things. Plants? Tiffany. Traps? Tiffany can show you. Tiffany's good at everything.

Tiffany's also really good at leaving an impression, it seems, because Taushen still views her as his perfect woman. Dark skin. Dark hair.

Damn it all, why do I care?

I shouldn't. I should feel sorry for him that he's in love with a happily mated woman. Instead, I just want to cheerfully choke someone at the thought of her smiling at him.

I told myself I didn't care. That we were just friends. But as I toss and turn in my bunk that night, I think it's pretty clear to me that we aren't—and can't be—just friends. Because I keep thinking about how sweetly he touched my hair and stroked my cheek as I lay under him. I think about the tender way he called me his mate. I think raunchier thoughts, too, like when he pulled my hair while he was deep inside me and I freaking loved it, and when his spur pushed against my back door and I loved that, too.

Really regretting my whole freakout and the "can we just be friends?" thing. This is new to me. It's not just that we're friends and I feel closer to him than I've ever felt to anyone. It's the added complication of him wanting more and me pushing him away and demanding nothing more than companionship. It was my choice, and he's given me what I wanted.

For all intents and purposes, he's moved on.

Me? I'm stuck. I keep thinking about that night and wondering if it was incredible because of the drugs or incredible because of the man. I won't know unless we have sex again. Because mind-blowing sex with my best friend? It might be the best thing ever. It might be...perfect. I might be in love.

But do I ruin what we've got by trying to push things in the direction of lovers once more? Or will he think I'm blowing hot and cold and get mad at me? If only he'd give me a signal of some kind, I could know which way to turn.

Of course, him telling me that Tiffany is his perfect woman *is* a signal. But I'm going to choose not to think of it that way. He liked me before. Maybe it was just his dick talking post-sex, but it's a shot. I can turn him from Tiffany, I think. She's mated and off the market, and I'm right here.

All I need to do is show him what he's missing out on. I think.

I hope.

19

TAUSHEN

"*W*here do you want to go next?" I ask Brooke the following morning. She is unusually quiet, purple smudges underneath her eyes that speak of a sleepless night. Does she worry over something? I want to make it better for her, and I itch to pull her against my chest and stroke her mane to comfort her. I want to protect her from the world, but I know that will only make her snarl at me and declare that she is fine and she does not need protecting. So I try a different tactic. "The great salt lake? Or somewhere else?"

"I suppose we should head in that direction soon," she muses, yawning and running a hand through her tangled mane. "Some-place with a bath. My hair feels grimy."

I chuckle. She is obsessed with her mane, my Brooke. And mine, too, come to think of it. There is not a day that passes that she does not take the opportunity to plait new designs in her mane and in mine. Today my mane has been dragged into two thick tails that twist into several smaller ones. It matters not to me, but she is pleased with the look. "If all you wish is a bath, there is a hot stream nearby."

She perks up. "Really?"

I nod. "We can go there after we eat, if you like."

"I'd love to. And then I guess we can head toward the ocean." She looks thoughtful. "How far away do you think we are?"

I shrug, because I can make the journey last as long as it needs to. "If we run the entire time, four days?"

Brooke stares at me. "How about if we take our time and sightsee and avoid running at all costs?"

I cannot help but grin at that. "Because you hate sweating?" It is another thing I have learned about Brooke. She makes unhappy noises when her body musk grows stronger and makes a big deal of washing her underarms every night and rubbing sweet-scented herbs on them. I think she smells lovely, but she does not wish to hear such things.

"Bitch, please. You try and run in snowshoes." She gives an adorably indignant snort. "Then we can talk about who's sweating and who's not."

"This bitch will be happy to take you for a bath, then."

A startled giggle bursts out of her, and my sac tightens in response. I am filled with longing for her. "Oh my god, that's so cute. You called yourself bitch."

"Should I not? You called me bitch." I move to the front of the cave to grab a bowlful of snow to toss onto the fire.

"Bitch is insulting, but lovingly so." Brooke chuckles.

"Humans have strange language." I ignore the way my heart

hammers at her description. Lovingly so. "Drink your tea fast, then, bitch."

"Oh boy. No, you can't use it like that."

"But—"

"Trust me. You can't call me bitch unless you're a girl...or you like cock. I guess it's all right then, too."

I scowl as I dump the snow onto the fire. "What does liking cock have to do with 'bitch'? I like my cock just fine. It is a very nice one."

"Oh, my sweet, innocent Taushen." She wiggles her eyebrows at me. "There are so many ways to answer that."

As we pack our things to leave the hunter cave, we continue talking. I tell her of my parents and their rare three-mating. I had two fathers, though only one resonated to my mother, and all three shared the furs together up until the khui sickness took them all from me. She is fascinated by how I had three parents and asks all kinds of questions, and it feels good to speak of them again, to share their memory with another. She tells me of her own childhood and how it was less happy. How her father was not mated to her mother and how her mother opened something called a "cray-deet card" in her name when she was a child and ruined her "cray-deet" before she was an adult. I do not understand what she means, but it is clear that she is unhappy about it. She tells me how she had no one to help her and yet she learned her trade of playing with manes and could make a living at it. There is pride in her voice as she speaks, and even though I do not understand the things she tells me about, I know it meant a lot to her.

I am about to tell her what a strong, brave female she is when she exclaims and puts a hand to her brow, peering ahead. "Is that the stream?"

"Likely." Though I want nothing more than to watch her expressive face, I turn my focus ahead, my spear in hand. I must ensure that the area is safe. Because there are fresh, running waters, that means there will be predators watching for a nearby dvisti herd or perhaps snowcats who approach to pluck the waiting fish curled against the bank, basking in the heat. Or worse, metlak, though we have not seen many on our journey. "Stay behind me," I caution her. "Keep a weapon at the ready just in case."

"Gotcha." She does not ask questions, just pulls out her small bone knife, a fierce expression on her face.

I move ahead, my spear in hand, ready to grab my belt-knife if I must. The snow here is fresh and untouched, though, not a single track other than the ones we make. I scan the area, but there is nothing, and no nearby overhanging cliffs where a snowcat can drop onto us. It seems to be safe enough. I cautiously approach the waters, seeing a few scattered fang-fish that have their feelers arching up from the water's surface.

"Clear," I tell her. "Let me ready the water for you." I take a handful of soapberries from my pouch and crush them in my hand, then scatter the sludge through the stream. After a moment, the fang-fish rouse from the banks and swim downstream, away from my location. It is something I have done time after time, but there is still a certain amount of satisfaction in watching them flee. I watch them go, and then turn to Brooke. "You can..."

Words die in my throat. I watch, mute, as Brooke strips her leathers off with slow, sensuous motions. She does not look at me, her eager gaze on the water.

"I'm so ready to bathe, you have no idea," she tells me, even as she flings aside her tunic into the snow, revealing only her small teat-supporting band that does not seem like enough leather to do its task.

I blink at her. For days on end, we have been careful around each other to ensure that we remain friendly. We dress under our furs, we give each other privacy when it is time to handle the body's needs, and we do not mention anything that would make the other uncomfortable.

So this is…unexpected.

It should not matter. My people are free with their bodies, and I have seen many—if not all—of the tribe in various states of undress. When you have a communal bathing pool, you see people, young and old, in nothing but their skin. But this is Brooke. Brooke, who makes sure her teats are covered at all times. Brooke, who smiles at me softly from the other side of the fire and asks me what my ideal mate looks like. Brooke, who told me I talked filthy even as she demanded I drive my cock into her.

Brooke, who holds my heart in her small, five-fingered hands and does not even realize it.

She reaches for the laces at the front of her teat-band and then pauses, tilting her head at me. "Are you going to wash up, too?"

It is strangely difficult to swallow. "Yes," I manage after a moment. But I need to wait until she turns away so she does not see how hard my cock is. Somehow I do not think she will see that as just friendship.

She turns her back to me with a little smile on her lips and undoes the band. Down it goes to the ground, and then she shimmies out of her long leather skirt, giving me a long look at her rounded, pink bottom. It is just as bouncy as her teats, and I am fascinated by the bareness of it and the way her hips swing as she saunters into the waters.

"So warm," she moans, and raises her arms above her head to her hair. I catch a glimpse of the side of one rounded teat as she does so, and then she sinks deeper into the waters.

I am sweating.

We are friends, I remind myself. Nothing more.

"Aren't you coming in? It feels so good."

"Soon." As soon as my cock goes down. Unfortunately, if she keeps using that sultry voice, it will not be happening speedily.

She turns her back to me, and I take the opportunity to rip my leathers off, practically tripping over my own two feet in my haste to get into the water. I manage to tumble in with a splash, but luckily my leathers do not follow me in. I hear Brooke's laughter as I push my sodden mane out of my eyes. "In a hurry?"

"Tripped," I tell her, lying.

Brooke puts her hand out, her teats barely hidden by the lapping water. "Soap?"

Ah. Yes.

I straighten and wade over to the bank, where I have more soap-berries in my pouch. Even as I do, I feel a hand grab ahold of my tail, and I nearly explode, on the verge of losing all control. "You going to clean this dirty thing?" Brooke teases. "Or you want me to do it for you?"

I close my eyes, because the thought of Brooke rubbing her hands up and down my tail is too much for this hunter to bear. "Fine. I am fine," I tell her thickly. "I can clean myself."

"Oh, fine," she says, a playful pout in her voice. "You're no fun."

"I am not," I agree. Not today. Not while I am thinking about things that a friend should not.

Brooke gives a sigh and takes a few soapberries from my outstretched hand, ignoring the pouch I offer her. She crushes them between her fingers and then raises her hands to her mane once more, and this time, I can almost see the pink tips of her teats as they rise out of the water.

It does not seem possible, but I am still sweating.

She is oblivious to reaction, though, her focus on her mane and then sweeping the suds up and down her arms. I have learned a lot about Brooke over the past turn of the moon. That her smiles do not always mean she wants something. Sometimes she is just playful. That she does her best to put me at ease, and that even when she is angry, her anger is fleeting and can be easily swayed with a small gift. She is full of love and happiness, my Brooke, and I crave her so much that it makes my spirit ache.

Now, I tell my khui. Look at how lovely she is. How her teats would be perfect to nurse a kit. How her smiles bring such joy. Does she not deserve a mate? Am I not the best one for her?

My khui does not agree, though, because it remains silent. Despair threatens to overwhelm me again. Why, of all the hunters, did I have to get the khui that wishes nothing more than to slumber in my breast? Why will it not claim a mate?

More importantly, why will it not claim Brooke? She is everything I have ever wanted and she holds my heart in her grasp. I need her. She should be mine.

"Wow, you're having some deep thoughts for a bath," Brooke's light, bubbling voice breaks into my thoughts. "You're frowning hard at those soapberries." She gives me another playful look, her mane nothing but spiky foam atop her head. "You should spend less time scowling and more time washing."

I nod and grab a few berries from the pouch, then toss the rest on the shore. With a squeeze, I crush the berries and then rub them up and down my arms furiously, then scrub at my face and horns, determined to forget about her. Forget about the need for a mate. I cannot dwell on what I cannot have, or I will go mad.

But then Brooke grabs at my tail again. "You're not washing." Her fingers trail up my tail and land at the small of my back, and I remain completely still in the hopes that she will put her hands in less...polite places. "You sure you're okay?"

What to say? That her touches make me crazed? That every morning, I contemplate flinging her down onto the furs and putting my mouth on her cunt until she grabs my horns and begs for more? That if she touches my tail again, I might not be able to control myself?

Then I will lose our friendship. I will have nothing of Brooke, not even her sweet smiles. She will hate me once more, and that I cannot bear.

"I am thinking about the great salt lake," I tell her instead. "And what Vektal will do to me when he finds I have stolen you away. He has had many, many nights to think about it."

"Oh stop," she tells me, and her hands slide up my back.

I stiffen, waiting. Waiting for her to touch me as a lover touches another. Waiting for her to give me a signal that yes, she wants to be more than friends.

But she only swipes at a fluffy pile of suds on my shoulder and begins to spread them across my skin, washing me. My Brooke, my mate in my heart, is washing my body.

It is the best thing I have ever felt and makes me hungry for so much more at the same time.

"Want me to do your front?" she asks, whispering in my ear.

If she does, I will not be able to control myself. "No," I choke out. "I do not."

She pauses, and then I hear her swim away. "All righty," she says, voice as cheery as ever.

I scrub at my skin hard, wondering if any male has ever been so tortured.

20

BROOKE

$\mathcal{W}$ as ever a man so clueless?

All afternoon, I've been testing the waters—so to speak—to see how Taushen would react if I flirted with him. To see if there's interest at all. And after an afternoon of tossing my hair, using my sultriest laugh, swinging my hips, and generally working him with my magic...

I have no freaking clue.

The man hasn't given me a single hint that he's attracted to me. He ignores my attempts to be sexy. He answers my teasing questions with brief, practically surly answers. And he completely shut me down in the stream earlier when I tried to make bathing sexy. Hell, I practically shoved my naked, wet tits in his face and all he did was scrub himself and look at the horizon like he was the most put-upon guy ever.

Gotta admit, it didn't do much for my ego.

It's weird because...I really thought he liked me. I have to admit it hurts my feelings that I can't get him to notice me. I've never had that problem in the past. I don't have a great face, but I do have large boobs and I know how to use 'em. In the past, I could get any guy to notice me. This one? I might as well be a nun.

It's all the more confusing because of our past together. I remember Taushen holding me close and declaring that I was his mate. I remember how he touched me. Has he...already moved on?

Jesus, the thought's a depressing one.

I'm not the kind of girl that gives up, though. That evening, when we set up a fire in a hunter cave, I watch his tail flick against the ground, over and over, like an annoyed cat. Hmm. I study him, but I can't tell what he's thinking. Is he annoyed at how things went in the stream earlier? Trying to be polite in the face of my cat-in-heat mentality? Wondering how to let me down gently?

Somehow that thought annoys me most of all, so I decide to try another tactic.

Sexy feeding.

It works in the movies, after all. I've never tried it before, but it'll allow me to watch his face this time, because scrubbing his back and guessing his expression didn't exactly get me places. Of course, what we're eating makes the "sexy" part a little more diffi-cult. I watch, wincing as Taushen cuts a slit into the belly of the quill-beast and then begins to carefully peel back the skin from the flesh, using his thumbs. Eeesh. Every time I see an animal skinned, it doesn't get any easier to put it in my mouth. It makes it doubly hard considering that the sa-khui like their meat raw.

Playing it safe never gets a girl anywhere, though. I tell myself that, even as he finishes skinning it and removes the organs so he can make a broth from them later. I wait for him to wash his hands and wipe them clean, and then he begins to cut our dinner into bite-sized chunks for cooking. Before he can skewer them, I put my hand on his. "Wait."

Taushen gives me a curious look. "What is it?"

"You've waited on me all day. I think it's time I return the favor."

"Eh?" He glances down at the food he's preparing and then back at me. "You wish to cook my food for me?"

"No, silly." I take the chunk of raw meat he's just cut and hold it up to his lips. "I'll feed you, though. You can just relax and enjoy." I make my voice drop to a sexy note and give him a winning smile, even as I press my arms against my sides so my tits plump out. "Sound good?"

"No." Taushen frowns at me, as if my brain has suddenly stopped working. "Why would you feed me like a kit?"

Like a kit? Seriously? "Oh stop. It's nice to have someone else take care of you, I promise. Just give it a try." I raise the food to his lips. "Take a little bite. Just a nibble...or you can use your tongue."

The look on his face is downright grumpy. "Or I can feed myself, like an adult would."

I keep smiling, though the urge to shove the food into his stupid face is getting stronger. This is supposed to be sexy, dammit. "Open up." I wiggle the bit of red meat at him, but it only causes a bit of the blood to roll down my hand and arm.

I'm going to ignore that, too.

Taushen grudgingly opens his mouth and I pop the food inside, making sure my fingers brush against his mouth as I do. I give him a seductive smile as he chews. "See, that wasn't so bad, was it?"

He shrugs his big shoulders, chewing slowly. "Is it supposed to change the taste if you feed me? It tastes the same."

Oh, for fuck's sake. "You know what? Never mind. Feed yourself."

"That is what I normally do. You make it sound like it is bad—"

I throw my arms up in the air and stalk outside to wash my hands in the fresh snow.

21

BROOKE

*W*hen I return to my seat, he gives me a curious look. "Are you well?"

"I'm fine," I tell him crabbily. I'm not all that fine, but I don't think he'd understand. It's clear he doesn't understand a lot of things.

"You say you are fine, but your tone says otherwise," he observes, cutting another chunk of meat off and holding it out to me. Not feeding me, just, well, *feeding* me. In an unsexy way. He hesitates when I don't take it from him. "Do you want this charred—"

"No. It's fine." I take the chunk of raw meat and pop it into my mouth, too defeated to even bitch that it's raw. I'll eat "sa-khui sushi" when the occasion calls for it, and right now I just don't even want to argue. Or talk. So I chew.

He continues to watch me, and after a long moment, goes back to carving the kill. "Do you wish to play a game?"

We normally play games around the fire at night. Charades always ends badly because his versions of words are different than mine, and it limits things when you can't use movies or actors or music. You can only guess "dvisti" so many times in a row before the game gets old. His favorite is I Spy, because it always works, and he finds it as delightful as I did when I was a child. Normally I think it's funny how competitive—and excited —he gets to play a child's game, but right now? I am so not in the mood. "Nope."

"We should. It will be good," he says, carving another hunk of meat and offering it to me. "I spy with my blue eye—"

"I told you. It's 'my little eye.'"

"My eyes are not little. Not like yours. So I will spy it with my blue eye. And I spy something red."

I'm going to ignore that crack about my eyes being little, because it wasn't meant in a shitty way. "Meat?"

"Yes! You are very good at this."

"Lucky me." I take another piece of food and chew thoughtfully. My turn. "Okay. I spy with my *little* eye...something brown." I do my best not to pointedly stare at his leather loincloth and give it away.

"Brown," he murmurs, glancing around the small cave. "Brown... is it my boot?"

"Nope." I take another bite of the gushy red meat.

"Is it...my waterskin?"

"Nope."

"Is it...the intestines of our dinner?"

Oh my god, are they *brown*? I look over at the pile of offal that's neatly covered by some folded leather. I can't see anything, but my imagination goes wild...and my stomach revolts. The mouthful I'm chewing on suddenly feels like it's gonna turn into vomit. "You know what? I'm done." And I rush to the front of the cave to spit out my food.

"What is it? What did I say?" Taushen calls after me. "Brooke?"

I don't answer. Too busy puking.

TAUSHEN

Brooke is in a bad mood for the rest of the evening. She does not eat, mends her clothes quietly, and will not play more games with me. When she decides to go to bed early, I do not protest. I do not like her bad mood, and I am fairly certain that I caused it. But I will deal with that tomorrow.

For now...I simply need to get away.

I wait in my furs, tense and aching as I listen to her breathing. Eventually it slows, and she drifts into sleep.

Finally.

I ease out of my bed silently, getting to my feet. It takes longer to move without sound, but I manage to creep through the cave without waking her, just as I do every night that we travel. I move out into the snow, wincing with every crunch of the powder under my toes. When I am satisfied I am far enough from the mouth of the cave for privacy, I glance around, checking to ensure that Brooke is not behind me.

Then, when I know I am alone, I quickly undo the laces on my loincloth and free my aching cock.

Every night, I have to leave and take myself into hand. I grip my shaft, stroking up and down quickly. I do not seek to prolong this; I just want relief.

Relief from Brooke's smiles, the subtle bounce of her teats with every step, the way she smells, the way she touched me in the stream. Her throaty laughter.

And her insistence that we be *friends*.

I will be as she wants. I will be her friend.

I will just take myself in hand every night to ensure that I do not lose control, that I do not do something foolish such as pulling her against me and kissing her. She has made it clear how she feels, and because I will take any small part of my Brooke that I can get, it will have to do.

So I stroke, imagining her pink mane tousled under me, her lips parted with pleasure as I ram into her cunt. The breath hisses from my throat as I imagine her teats jiggling as I thrust into her, the little cries she makes. It does not take long, not when I imagine her. A growl breaks from my throat, and my seed, thin and clear, spurts over my hand and fingers as I stroke. I wring every last bit of pleasure from the furtive touch and then shake my hand, flinging my discarded seed into the snow.

The sight of it makes me bitter. Not because she has turned me away. It is her choice, and I understand it. It is because I cannot control myself around her. She washed my back earlier today and my cock immediately rose. How can we possibly remain friends if I cannot control myself around her?

I worry I will ruin everything.

22

BROOKE

*I*t's clear I'm going to have to be more obvious.

I think about it all the next day and into the night, when I'm lying in my furs pretending to sleep. Dinner was tense, with Taushen shooting me questioning looks with every bite he ate. I went to bed immediately afterward, but I haven't slept. I'm just lying there, staring into the darkness, trying to figure him out.

He said I was his mate.

He's pushed me away ever since.

He might be afraid to make the first move.

Or he just might be happy that we're friends and he's dreaming of one of the sixteen girls back at camp. Maybe it's not Tiffany that's my competition, but a dark-skinned beauty sleeping in the pods even now.

Fuck.

Why am I so stupid? Why did I fall for a guy promptly after I friendzoned him? Is it me? Am I the problem here? Can I just not be happy with what I have?

I've tried, I really have. It's just that every time he smiles at me, or teases me, I feel this deep, sweet ache inside. I want more. I want him to touch me again. I want to wake up with his arms around me. I want to know that I've got a partner in this crazy world that I've found myself in. I want him deep inside me.

And I can't bear the thought that I'm the only one that might want this.

I don't give up, though. I never give up. It's time to be slightly more obvious. Obvious in such a way that it actually makes me cringe a little, because any Earth guy would see what I'm doing coming from a mile away...but Taushen's not an Earth guy. He's woefully clueless, so I'm going to have to be that much more forward.

So I toss and turn in my bed, pretending my sleep is restless and awful. I let this go on for a minute, and then I sit bolt upright with a little cry.

"Brooke?" Taushen's at my side in an instant, his hand on my shoulder. "What is it?"

"A horrible nightmare," I whisper, turning and burying my face against his chest. "It was so awful!" I cling to him, waiting to see his reaction. If he just gives me a pat on the back and tells me to go back to sleep, I'm going to scream in frustration.

To my delight, he puts his arms around me, zero hesitation in him. "I have you," he tells me, and one big hand strokes my hair tenderly. I could weep at how sweet he is, how thoughtful. He holds me close until I stop fake-shivering, and even after that, seems content to let me snuggle against him.

I take greedy advantage of it, too. He's so warm and he smells fantastic—like soapberry and musk and big sexy male and all the good things I love. I want him so badly I could cry. Why did I ever think we should be just friends? I should have taken that night of fantastic sex—drugs or no—and told him that I wanted it again, but this time without coercion. That this time I'd touch him and it'd be because I wanted to, not because some goofy drink was making me. That it could still be just as good in every way. No, better. Better because this time I truly wanted it and him.

Instead, I have to play silly games to make him realize I've changed my mind. I sigh.

"I should let you go," he says, misinterpreting my sigh. He pulls away. "You—"

"No," I say quickly, and cling to him like a baby monkey. "I'm afraid I'll have more bad dreams. Stay with me?"

He hesitates.

I slide under the blankets again and hold on to his arm, patting the furs with my other hand. "You can lie right next to me. There's room for both of us, I promise."

I'm afraid for a moment that Taushen will see through my oh-so-obvious ploy and call me out on it, but he only nods and slides in next to me. His feet brush against my leg, and then I can feel his tail flick against my thigh, as if he's making sure that I'm really okay with this. I resist the urge to grab it and tuck it between my thighs, because that would be dirty and wrong.

I mean, I still want to do it, because I love me some dirty and wrong.

Taushen's arms go around me and he pulls me back against his chest, and for a moment, I'm just lost in how good it feels to press up against him. I'm enveloped in a full-body hug and I love it. So good. I close my eyes and pillow my head against his hard chest.

"Are you comfortable?" he asks softly, and I can feel his hand stroke up and down my arm, rubbing it.

"I'm great," I tell him, even though those small touches are making me get a little damp between my thighs.

"Go back to sleep, then. I will hold you and make all the bad dreams disappear," he tells me, and his tail strokes my thigh.

God, he's killing me with how sweet he is. I want to eat him alive. For now, though, I'll just settle for putting my hand on his hard abdomen and sighing happily. "Right. Back to sleep."

I'm quiet—though not sleepy—for several minutes while he continues to stroke my arm and hold me close. I try to keep my breathing even so he doesn't suspect I'm awake.

And then I slowly inch my hand down, lower.

I'm sleeping in nothing more than my tunic top, because it gets too warm at night for leggings and boots both. I don't have panties or my leather bra-band on either, and I'm going to use that to my advantage. I give another heavy sigh as if I'm sleeping and then hook my leg between his, more or less pushing his knee between my thighs.

And I slide my hand even lower, until it's resting on the band of his loincloth. It's the only thing he's wearing, and for a moment, I wish he was sleeping naked. So, so naked. But I can work with this. I yawn, and then slide my hand right onto his crotch.

He's hard as a rock, and huge.

Yes. He's not made of stone, after all. Friendship, my ass. This man wants me.

Taushen sucks in a breath. For a moment, he doesn't breathe—and damn it all if it doesn't make it that much harder to pretend that I'm asleep—and then, carefully, pulls my hand off his junk.

Damn it.

I continue pretending to sleep, smacking my lips and rubbing up against him. I put my hand back on his stomach again, and when he relaxes, put it back on his hard cock once more.

"Brooke?" he asks, voice low. "What are you doing?"

"Mmm?" I am such a terrible actress, because I don't sound sleepy even to my own ears. I lightly rub his cock through his leathers, my pulse pounding. I'm definitely wet now, and hungry for more touching.

"What is it you are doing?" he asks again, and pulls my hand off his cock once more. "You are not sleeping, are you?"

Found out. Damn it. I decide to plow ahead with my plan. I turn my face toward his skin and nuzzle his nipple, then lick it with my tongue.

The breath hisses from his lungs, and I have to bite back my moan of breathless excitement. In the next moment, though, my moan turns to frustration because he pushes me away, scooting backward in the furs. "What is it you do, Brooke?"

This isn't exactly how I envisioned this going. I was hoping it'd have more sexy humping and less accusation. "I'm trying to seduce you," I say playfully. "Let's have sex." And I put my hand boldly on his cock again.

He grabs me by the wrist and stares down at me. "I do not understand."

"I dunno, I thought I was being pretty obvious," I mutter.

"You said you wished to only be friends!"

"Yeah, well, maybe I changed my mind? I'm allowed to do that!" I jerk my hand back from him, my frustration bubbling to the surface. "You're really hard to freaking read, you know? I've been throwing myself at you over and over and all I get is blank looks. I don't know if those blank looks mean you're not interested or you're just clueless. Maybe it was wishful thinking on my part that you'd still be interested, but you can just tell me outright, you know. I can take a hint. And if you—"

He flings me onto my back on the furs, cutting off my words. His intent face looms over mine, a scarce inch from my nose. Taushen's curious gaze devours me. "You...have been trying to get my attention?"

"Uh, duh? Washing your back? Feeding you? I figured since that wasn't direct enough I'd just grab your dick, but even that didn't seem to work." My hurt feelings are surfacing, and I push at him. "Get off me."

"No." His lips twitch with amusement.

"I'm serious. You may think this is funny, but I don't." I actually kind of feel like crying with disappointment. "I get it. The window has passed. I snoozed, I, uh, losed. You can let a girl down easy. I—"

His mouth covers mine.

23

BROOKE

I'm so startled that I don't even kiss him back. He's... kissing me? But I thought he was shocked that I'd touched him. I thought he didn't want anything to do with me. "What," I murmur as his lips slick against mine and his hand goes to my waist. "Taushen..."

"You said," he murmurs between kisses, "'I wish to be friends, Taushen. It was not me that craved your touch that night.'" Over and over, his mouth dips over mine, until it's hard to concentrate on what he's saying. "You said that you wanted no mate. You said—"

I grab him by his ears and hold his face an inch away from mine, breathless. I need a moment to think. "I also said 'Pull my hair, you dirty freak'. I say a lot of things."

As if I'm telling him to do that right now, he slides a hand into my hair and grabs a loose fistful and...I don't hate it. I swallow back a

whimper of delight. It's like his big hand in my hair just emphasizes how strong he is, how brutal, and yet he's so utterly gentle
with me. It's the contrast between the two that makes me insane
with lust.

"If you say so many things, then tell me you wish to be my mate,"
he demands, leaning in and brushing his lips over mine
once more.

"I want to be your mate," I tell him, grabbing a handful of his
long hair and twisting it around my fingers. "Mine and only mine.
No looking at other women. Not Tiffany, not any of the new
chicks. Eyes firmly on me. I'm possessive like that."

He presses a light kiss to the tip of my nose, and I nearly melt into
goo at the sweetness of that little gesture. "I have not looked at
another female since you touched me."

"Really?"

"Really." He kisses lightly across my brows.

"Then what was all that, 'Oh, my perfect woman is brown-haired
and brown-skinned and blah blah blah—"

"Because if I said my perfect female has pink hair and pink-
tipped teats, that would tell you that I wished to be more than
friends, would it not? And I was doing my best to be a friend." He
chuckles, his warm breath fanning across my face. "It was very
hard. I have stroked my cock many nights in agony."

"You have? Why didn't I see this?" Damn, I would have watched
that for years.

"You were too busy snoring—" At my indignant squeal, he breaks
off into laughter. "I have lived in a village full of others all my life.
I share a hut with many other males. You think I cannot stroke

my cock quietly? I have become an expert at using my palm in silence."

"That is a terrible thing to tell a chick when you're making out with her," I say to him, letting my fingers tickle up and down his side. He's smiling at me, so big and happy and carefree, and his words are so teasing...I'm just utterly fascinated. I think of what Harlow said before, how happy Taushen used to be. Is this the man he's supposed to be? Teasing and full of joy?

If so, I completely approve.

"Is there a different way to tell a female you have stroked your cock? Is there a game I do not know? Perhaps more I Spy?" His eyes gleam with enthusiasm, and he pulls at the laces of my tunic. "I spy with my blue eye...something that is about to come off of my female."

I can't help but laugh at that. "Is it...the blanket?"

"No. Guess again." He tugs the laces free and then makes a noise of frustration when he realizes it won't actually remove my tunic. "How does this come off?"

"Over my head. Want me to do it?"

"Let me." His eyes gleam with excitement. "I wish to undress my mate and lay her down into my furs."

They're my furs, but I'm not going to spoil his fun on a technicality. "All right." I sit up, and when he pulls on the hem of my tunic, I obediently raise my arms so he can take my tunic off. The moment it whisks over my hair, I'm completely and utterly naked in front of him. I'm practically quivering, imagining his reaction. Is he going to stare at my boobs? Touch me? What?

Instead, he gazes into my eyes and touches my cheek. I think he's trying to caress me, but when I close my eyes, he taps my chin. "Look at me."

"What is it?" I give him a curious look.

"This is you asking for this? This is not...a bad drink? It is my Brooke, and her thoughts are clear?"

The fuck? Is he asking if I got drunk to sleep with him? I start to get angry that he would even ask such a thing, but I pause and bite the words back. Even if it's a little bit offensive, I can understand where he's coming from. After last time, I don't blame him for asking.

And there is so much hope and wariness in his expression, as if he's afraid that it's all just a trick or a dream and the rug's going to be pulled out from under him once more. My heart aches for him. He wants this—wants me—so bad. It's humbling and flattering at the same time.

For a second, I feel like the most powerful woman ever. I hold this gorgeous, fierce, strong man in the palm of my hand. It's a heady gift, and one I intend to cherish.

"This is your Brooke," I tell him softly. "No roofies, no Spanish fly, no drugs, no alcohol. Just me, happy that I finally get to touch you like I've been dreaming about for days." And I put my hand on his chest, over the hard plating that covers his heart.

"Bah. Days? It has been days?"

"Several." I give him an impish grin.

He makes an irritated sound in his throat even as he tenderly covers my hand with his. "To think of all the times I could have touched you instead of using my hand...you make a hunter weep, Brooke."

"I'll make it up to you," I tell him flirtily. "Should we play more I Spy? I spy something that should come off of *my* mate."

"Your mate?" His grin is huge and proud.

"Yep, all mine. No takebacks." I smile at him, loving his happiness. Is it possible for a big blue hunk of delicious man to be a ray of sunshine? I feel like he's turning into one, and I adore it.

"Very well." He glances down, checking his body, but he's only wearing one thing—a very small loincloth that looks like it's not big enough to hold all the drama behind it. "This?"

"That," I agree with satisfaction. "It needs to come off."

I've never seen a man undress so fast. The laces fly through the air, and then the loincloth is flung across the room, and Taushen's kneeling in front of me in all his blue glory. After weeks of carefully trying not to get naked around each other, seeing all this bare skin feels utterly decadent, and I sit up, unable to stop from putting my hands on him to explore.

"I get to touch you, right?" I whisper.

"As long as I get to touch you."

"Of course." I flex my fingers, looking him up and down. There is so much to look at, too. Acres and acres of blue muscles covered by the softest, fuzziest skin. Tight, thick thighs and an equally tight bubble of a butt. A dick that goes on for days.

Spur.

Tail.

This is a damn horndog buffet, and I intend on going back for seconds. "Mmm. Shall I go first, or should we do it at the same time?"

"We can touch at the same time," he murmurs, and I feel something flutter up the back of my thigh, then graze my butt cheek. His tail.

Oh, that is so cheating. Naughty, naughty, filthy man. I can't help the little moan that escapes me. Of course, now he's ahead of me in the touching, so I plant both my hands on his chest and contemplate where to go first. Appetizers? Main course? Head straight for dessert?

Go slow, I think. Pace yourself. Enjoy.

I put my hand on one bicep and squeeze. It's rock hard, and I can't put my hand around it. Hell, I can't even circle it with both hands, and the thought just makes me all fascinated and aroused. How is it that I've been around this man for weeks and I've never realized how big his guns are? Or that touching him feels like touching the softest velvet ever? I sigh happily. "I don't know where to touch first."

"It does not matter to me," he says, and then drags me against his chest so he can nibble on my neck. All the while, his tail continues to flick against my thigh and bottom, almost as if he's petting me.

Doesn't matter where I touch him, hmm? That sounds like a challenge if I ever heard one. I let my hands wander down his chest, stroking over his nipples, and I'm disappointed when I don't get a huge response. Maybe those aren't sensitive like mine are. I rub up against him, desperate to feel his skin against mine. Does his skin feel as incredible against my nipples as it does under my fingers?

Oh god, yes it does.

I moan, moving back and forth to drag my nipples against his chest. It might possibly be the best thing I've ever felt. He pulls me closer, his hands roaming up and down my back. "Brooke. My Brooke. This feels like a dream."

"It's real," I tell him, feeling a surge of absurd happiness. "What we have is real, I promise." I move my hands down to his shaft, caressing him. I didn't imagine those ridges, then, or just how big his spur is. It seems strange to have such a piece of anatomy, but when I lightly run my fingers over it and feel his shiver of response, I remember how good it felt sliding through the slick folds of my pussy.

Weird or not, I can't wait to experience it again.

He nips at my throat once more and then lifts his head, giving me a heated look. "We did not finish our game."

"We didn't?"

Taushen shakes his head. "I spy with my blue eye..." His big hand smooths down my shoulder, across my collarbones, and then moves to cup one of my breasts. "Something pink that is about to go into my mouth."

"Hope it isn't my hair," I tell him, breathless.

He just gives me a playful look—oh god, he's so playful, and that's so damn sexy—and then puts both of his hands behind my back. I'm about to protest that I want my pink things in his mouth when he leans in to kiss me, and I can feel him gently guiding me down onto my back in the furs.

I lie back, arching as I do, because I know it thrusts my breasts into the air. I'm shameless like that; I want him to pet them. I want his mouth nipping at them, his lips on my skin. "What do you spy now?"

"My mate," he says thickly, and oh god, that makes me so wet.

I moan, reaching for him. "How are you so sweet and so filthy at the same time?"

"I am not filthy," he murmurs, and lowers his head between my breasts. His horns are practically in my face, but I don't care. I just want his mouth on my nipples. "My mate washed me, remember?"

"All I remember is washing you and being frustrated that you didn't pounce on me the moment I put my hands on you." His mouth closes over one nipple, and I gasp, whimpering at the delicious sensation.

"Clever," he murmurs. "I did not realize."

"That much was obvious."

He mock-growls at my tone and cups my breast in one hand, his mouth descending back down on the other. "It does not matter. You have me now."

I sure do. I love it, too. I love the way his big body feels over mine, the way his teeth oh-so-gently scrape over my nipple, the way he teases my other breast with his thumb. It makes me positively crazy, and I want him to stay there forever.

But then he lifts his head and gives me a playful, heavy-lidded look that promises so many naughty things. "I spy with my blue eye something I should put my mouth on."

And then he begins to kiss lower on my belly.

Screw the boobs. Did I want him to stay there? I want him to go south. A big, sexy man willing to do oral is like a unicorn in my experience, and if he's willing, I'm going to take him up on the offer.

24

BROOKE

*P*anting, I lift my hips, encouraging him down. Hell, I'll put my hand on his head and push him farther down if that's what it takes. "You can do anything to me," I tell him encouragingly. "I'll like all of it, I promise."

"They say there is no taste sweeter than the cunt of a mate," he whispers, kissing a trail down my belly.

"Do they say that? God bless your ancestors." I wriggle underneath him, impatient. "They knew exactly what they were talking about."

"I have dreamed about tasting you," he tells me, moving lower down my belly. His lips tickle my skin. "Dreamt of what you would smell like when I parted your folds. Last time, you did not let me touch you here, remember?"

It's all a haze, but I vaguely remember something along those lines. "I must have been crazy to turn that down."

"I am glad," he says, and lifts his head to gaze at me with steady, intense blue eyes. "We saved it for now. It will be special that we experience it together and your head is clear."

I'm melting at his sweetness...and impatient for him to talk less and use that tongue in other ways. "Me too."

His hand presses over my heat, and then he looks up at me, as if checking to make sure I'm okay with this. Oh boy, am I *ever* okay with this. To show him just how okay I am with it, I slide one leg over his shoulder and dig my heel into his back. "Touch me, Taushen."

My barbarian groans low, and his mouth is so close to the curls over my sex that I can feel his breath. It sends a shiver arching through my body. "I want to savor this," he tells me. "Tell me if I do it in a way that does not please you."

I don't think that's possible, but I reach down and touch his cheek. "I will. You don't have to do this, you know. Not every man wants to touch a woman there—"

He gives me a look like I'm talking crazy. "I want this more than anything."

Which is good, because I want his mouth there more than anything. "All right. I'm just letting you know that if it's not your thing, I understand—"

My words die in a squeak because he lowers his head and licks me. Just flat out licks my pussy like I would lick an ice cream. It's ticklish and startling and I squirm, waiting for him to do more. He looks up at me to check that I'm still okay with things, and then lowers his head again.

This time, it's a more exploratory lick. He parts my folds, licks me long and slow, and then growls low in his throat. "They were right," he murmurs. "You taste like nothing I have experienced before."

"I guess that's a good thing," I say nervously, feeling a little on edge at this thorough perusal. "I mean, if it tasted like quill-beast, hunters would be bringing those back all day long and we'd be super tired of it—"

Laughter breaks from him, and he gives me a startled, pleased grin, his mouth wet with my juices. And the sight of him like that makes my heart give a crazy little flip. I love this man.

"Do you distract me from my game?" he murmurs, flattening one big hand over my belly and dipping his thumb into my navel, as if fascinated by it. "Because I am not finished. I have only started."

I shiver at the promise in that. "Not distracting," I whisper. "Go ahead." I reach out and caress his cheek again, just because I want to touch him.

Taushen grins at me like I've given him a gift, and then his mouth lowers again. I feel his tongue slick along my folds, exploring. He takes his time tasting me, and I try to hold as still as possible so I don't derail him once more. I concentrate on other things, like his tail flicking back and forth against my leg, the press of his body on my thighs, the strands of his long, black hair that fan over my lower half. The soft sounds he makes that tell me he's enjoying himself.

I'm so fixed on him that I'm startled when his tongue flicks against my clit. It sends a rush of pleasure through my body, and I make a startled noise.

He lifts his head, and the look on his face is so pleased and smug that I nearly laugh. "Third nipple," he says, a triumphant note in his voice.

"Third...*what*?" What on earth is he talking about?

I open my mouth to ask what he means exactly, but then he lowers his head again and drags his tongue over my clit with renewed enthusiasm. A cry is wrested from my throat, and I forget all about not moving and not distracting him. Fuck distraction. "More," I pant, breaking my vow not to push down on his head. I plant a hand there and guide him back between my thighs. "You're doing amazing, Taushen. You're...ooooh. Oh god, you're really good at this."

It feels like my eyes are going to roll back in my head if he keeps going like that, too. What he lacks in finesse and expertise, he makes up for with enthusiasm and a ridged tongue. Those two things combined? It's maddeningly delicious, and I quickly lose all control. Within moments, I'm panting along with every swipe of his tongue, moaning in frustration when he changes his rhythm, and curling my fingers in his thick hair, need overtaking me.

I'm surprised when the orgasm bursts through me, because he hasn't even used his fingers yet. I've come just from licking alone, and I've come *hard*. I cry out his name, shuddering with the ferocity of it all.

He lifts his head, a smug look on his big, handsome face. "I want to do it again."

Panting, I put a hand to my forehead. "Give a girl a moment to catch her breath. Jesus."

The expression on his face turns from masculine superiority to boyish pleasure. "I pleased you, then?"

"Oh god, yeah." I sigh happily, still breathless. "Pleased doesn't seem to be the right word." Wrecked might be better.

"Good." He lowers his head again, ready to go for round two.

I grab his horns before he can. "Wait," I tell him. "I need longer than that. My toes still haven't uncurled."

He looks a bit disgruntled at my lack of stamina and slides back up next to me, caressing my breasts. "Tell me when you are ready again. I am eager for more."

It's hard to concentrate when he's playing with my boobs. I'm trying to catch my breath, but he seems fascinated with my nipples, toying with them in gentle, maddening ways that soon have me squirming and panting all over again. When I can't stand it any longer, I roll onto my side, fling my arms around his neck, and take him down in a fierce kiss.

Taushen chuckles against my mouth, rolling us again until I'm underneath him, and his tongue slicks into my mouth. Cruel thing. So much for letting a girl rest. I'll complain later, I decide. Much later. His tongue tangles with mine, and he strokes one hand down my body, and I want more than just this. I want everything.

And as he reaches for my breast again, I realize I want to blow his mind. I want to make him come as hard as I just came. An idea strikes, and I suck in a breath. Do I dare? Will he think me awful and slutty? Or will he love it?

He pulls back, a curious look on his face. "What is it?"

"Just wondering if you want to try something a little...naughty." I bite my lip and give him my most winning smile.

"Is it...acceptable?" He cups my breast. "Do I get to touch you?"

"Oh yeah." I chuckle at the thought. "You get to touch me a lot."

"Then show me."

"You have to promise me you won't think I'm sleazy if we do this, though."

"Slee-zee?" He frowns. "What is this word?"

Ugh. Having to explain everything makes it somehow ten times worse. "It's where you think I'm a bad person because I have more experience in the furs than you." I inwardly cringe, waiting to hear his response. Truth of the matter is, I do have a lot more experience in the furs than he does. I've had my share of poor choices and regrettable one-night stands. I've had boyfriends where I thought I was in love and I've had stupid, meaningless flings. I'm a normal modern girl. But what if that's too much for him? What if he finds the thought appalling? I hold my breath, waiting for him to say something. Anything.

His expression grows concerned, and I swear I feel my heart breaking into a million pieces. "Brooke," he says softly. "I do not have such experience. I do not wish for you to think less of me because I am no expert in the furs."

"No. That's silly. Why would I think less of you?" I give him a teasing smile. "That just means you're trainable."

He doesn't smile back. "Then it is not a flaw in your eyes?"

"Only if you don't find it a flaw that I've been with other men."

Taushen's expression darkens. "I do not like the thought of another male touching you. Touching what is mine."

"That's the past, though," I tell him softly. "You're my future."

He nods and leans in close to me for another kiss. "And that is all that matters."

I kiss him ferociously at those words. Most guys are not so understanding, but then again, I've always known that Taushen isn't like anyone else. Even on this planet, he holds himself just a little differently than the rest. I love him for it. "I adore you," I tell him, caressing his cheek.

"You have my heart, my Brooke." He nuzzles me gently, lips caressing mine.

"Can I do something naughty to you now?" I ask, wanting to blow his mind like I've been dreaming about.

"You can do anything you like to me," he says, skimming his thumb over my lower lip, as if fascinated by my mouth.

"Good. Do you have lotion? Or oil?"

That makes him pause. "Oil?"

"Something you'd put on your leather, maybe? Or lotion for your hands to stop them from drying out?"

"Yes...but why?"

"I'll show you." I give him my most sultry smile and put my hand out, palm first. "Lotion, please."

He shoots me a curious look but gets up and stalks over to his furs, bending over gracefully to pick up his travel bag. I can't help but ogle the tight buns he's packing, and the slowly flicking tail. We're definitely going to have to think up some naughty scenarios for that tail...later. Tonight, I'm bringing all the naughty.

He strides back to my side with one of the hollowed, tiny horns in hand, and offers it to me as he sits back down once more. I take it, curious to see that it's an ointment of some kind. "What's this for?"

"Chapped hands. I took it from the supplies. Har-loh has extra. Rukh says her hands get dry when they travel."

So he was thinking of me? That's sweet. I can't help but smile at the thought, and I offer it back to him. "This'll be more fun if you do the honors."

"Honors?" Taushen gives me a blank look. "What do you mean?"

"I need you to lotion me up."

"Ah." He still looks confused. "Very well, give me your hand."

"Not my hands," I say, and then crawl forward. I slide into his lap and put my arms around his neck. "You're going to lotion my tits."

I love the hiss of breath that escapes him. "Why?"

Why? I giggle at his question. "Because we're going to make them all slick." I reach for his cock. "And then I'm going to lotion this and make it all slick. And then you're going to put your cock between my breasts and..."

His low groan drowns out my words. "Humans do that?"

"The fun ones do." I can't stop smiling. "Wanna be fun?"

"More than anything."

"Want me to go first, then?" I take the little pot from him and get out a fingerful of the lotion. I slather it over my hands, making sure that my movements are slow and sensual. Then I lean in to kiss him, and as I do, I slide my slick hands up and down his cock, greasing up his length.

He remains frozen against me, his lips parted, as if he can't kiss and think at the same time. I stroke him over and over, my fingers moving up and down the ridges and caressing every inch of him. He's glorious, and I love that he's mine.

"Ready for your turn?" I whisper to him.

That jolts him out of his trance. He eagerly grabs the pot from me and rubs a dollop onto his hands, his gaze on my breasts. I sit up straighter, letting them jut out for his approval. I love that he's so fascinated with them. It's different when Taushen ogles my breasts than when human guys do. There's no creepiness in his stare, only appreciation.

Then his hands are on me, and it feels so good, so right. The slick caress of his touch is incredible, and I moan aloud as his fingers move over my breasts. He rubs the lotion on them with tender, slow strokes, brushing over my nipples repeatedly. I wasn't prepared for how good that would feel, and I'm rocking up and down against his body, rubbing up against him. If he wasn't covered in lotion, I'd have already climbed on top of him and sunk him deep inside me, but it's too late for that. I'll pleasure him, and then that will be enough, for now.

We have the rest of our lives to explore everything else.

"Ready?" I whisper to him, and take him in hand again. Our lips meet in a delicate kiss, and he nods.

Perfect.

"Stand up for me," I tell him, and when he does, I realize he's too tall. His cock is the perfect height for my mouth, but not for my breasts. I glance around the cave and then grab the nearest stool, settling onto it and then pulling him forward. This time, my height is perfect, and I cup my breasts, forming a tight valley between them. I gaze up at him, smiling. "Give me your cock, Taushen."

He groans, and his hand goes to my shoulder as he steps forward. It takes a little maneuvering for both of us, but I refuse to feel awkward. I love him. He loves me. Nothing we do together is strange. His tail wraps around my upper arm, and then he pushes his cock between my breasts. He pumps once, and I squeeze them tighter together, trying to create the right feel for him.

"Incredible," Taushen breathes, and the look of ecstasy on his face is worth it. It's worth everything.

"I wanted to do this for you," I tell him. "Because now when you look at my tits, you're going to think of this."

He groans again and thrusts between my breasts once more. He starts a rhythm, slow and teasing, and I watch, fascinated as the head of his cock pops in and out between my breasts, temptingly close to my mouth. The lotion has provided enough lubricant that we're both slippery in the best kind of way, though I'm getting wet all over again and turned on. As he thrusts, he reaches down and begins to toy with my nipples, and then I'm going crazy, too.

By the time he comes, I'm a panting, needy mess. I don't care that he comes all over my breasts, painting them with his release. I just want more of him. When he catches his breath, he grabs his tunic and mops at my skin, and it takes him a moment to realize that I'm flushed with need and breathing hard.

Takes about two seconds for him to topple me onto my back and for his face to go between my legs again. Doesn't take long for me to come again, either. I'm screaming his name while he licks me feverishly, and by the time we're both sated, I feel sweaty, a little sticky, and I'm pretty sure my hair is greasy from the lotion.

He pulls me against him in the furs and tucks me under his chin, pressing a kiss to my forehead. His tail slips around my thigh, locking me close. "I think we should go back to the bathing pool in the morning."

I chuckle. "I think you're right."

25

TAUSHEN

*M*y mate. I scarcely believe this is real.

I have dreamed of this for so long that I do not know what to think. Some small part of me is terrified that I will awaken and find that it is all a dream...so I do not go to sleep. I hug my mate close and breathe in her scent as she slumbers. I stroke her hair back from her face and watch her. I want to mate her again, but she needs her rest.

There will be time, I have to remind myself. It is hard to think that way, when I feel every moment slipping between my fingers. I feel such joy that Brooke is mine...and then I remember she is meant to resonate to another.

She wants to head to the ocean, rejoin the others.

If I take her there, she will resonate to one of the other males. I should tell her, but she will be angry that I kept such a thing from her. Yet how can I lie? More than anything, I want her happiness, but the thought of another male touching her, of her going from my furs to another's, makes me crazed with jealousy.

I hold her close and press my lips to her mane.

Perhaps I will take her...an indirect route, allow us more time to be together. Allow myself more time to think of an alternate plan of some kind.

She wakes sometime after dawn, and I heat water for her so we can bathe. The stream is ideal, but it is also too far away and she wants to clean up before we head out. So we wash by the fire, and I try not to stare as she moves the soapy scrap of leather between the teats that I rubbed my cock between last night. It was such a strange yet pleasing thing to do. She is right; every time she walks past and her teats jiggle, I am going to imagine her below me, pressing them around my cock as I thrust between the slick mounds.

I grow hard just thinking about it even now. But Brooke has given no indication that she wishes to touch this morning, and I do not know how mated couples handle such things. Do I grab her and kiss her? Show her that I would be happy mating right now? Or should I be patient and wait for her to tell me when she is ready again?

A splash catches my attention. I look up, just in time to see Brooke toss her leather washcloth into the pouch of heated water. She flings herself at me, arms going around my neck, and kisses me passionately. "Good morning," she hums low in her throat, giving me a sultry smile.

I kiss her fiercely, and then we descend into the furs. It seems she wants a mating as much as I do, and instead of leaving the cave that day and heading on the trails, we remain in our bedding. Brooke wraps her legs around me and pulls me close, encouraging me to sink into her. I guide my shaft to her cunt and find that she's wet and ready. When I push into her, she feels so good I nearly come in a matter of moments. I hold on to her, panting, and she tells me to go ahead. That she wants all of my touches, even quick ones.

The first time I come, I do not last long. I make it up to her with kisses and caresses, and when we mate a second time, I'm able to make her scream her release twice before I take mine.

The third time is even better.

After that, our matings begin to run together in one endless stream of twined limbs and sweaty skin. I barely notice that time is passing, until Brooke begins to shiver under me, and I realize she is cold and the fire has gone out. I light it again, warm food for her, and this time I let her feed me. Her fingers graze my fangs as she gives me tidbits, and I realize just how enticing this can be.

We do not last long before we return to the furs.

The next morning, I wake my mate with my mouth on her sweet cunt, and I do not let her free before she has come twice. I cover her, our mouths locked, and we both come a third time together. Panting, she pushes me away and crawls toward the fire. "Water," she whispers, pretending to rasp. "So. Dehydrated. Need. Water."

I chuckle at her dramatics, locking my tail around her ankle. "Do not leave for long."

She gives me a playful look over her shoulder and tips back her waterskin, draining it before tossing it aside and reaching for mine. "Shouldn't we be heading out soon?"

Her words strike fear into my heart. "Heading out?" I echo, pretending I do not understand.

Brooke yawns, sipping my waterskin and then offering it to me. I take it, but my concentration is entirely on her. "Yes. I thought we

were going to make our way toward the ocean? Meet the others?"
She crawls back into bed next to me and tucks her cheek against
my shoulder.

I make my voice as casual as I can. "Perhaps we will stay here
another day or two. You are tired."

She pokes me in the side, giggling. "No more tired than you. Are
you stalling? Do you not want to see the others?"

I am silent.

Brooke sits up, resting on one elbow, and gives me an incredulous
look. "You *are* stalling. What's going on?"

The words knot in my throat. Do I tell her the truth and risk
losing her? But she is my mate. She has my heart. How can I keep
such things from her?

She reaches over and grabs my chin, turning my face so my gaze
meets hers. "Taushen? You're scaring me. Spit it out."

"My mate is so beautiful," I tell her, touching her face.

Brooke swats my hand away. "Nuh-uh. Either you tell me what's
going on or you get to start making love to your hand again."
There's a frustrated, frightened tone in her voice. "What's
wrong?"

I have to tell her. "I stole you away from the others because I
wished to mate you."

"Duh. In other news, water is wet." She rests one arm casually on
my stomach, lounging across me. Her teat presses against my
skin, and I feel another powerful surge of lust. It seems impossible that I should want her so fiercely again after mating so
many times in the last few hours. "What's the real problem?" she
asks, dragging my thoughts back.

"I...stole you. Rokan said that you would resonate soon. I stole you to keep you with me."

She blinks. "Resonate soon? Me?"

I nod, suddenly consumed by jealousy. I tug her down against me. "You are mine, Brooke. You do not belong to another!"

"Whoa, whoa," she says, pulling away from me. There's a tiny smile playing on her mouth. "You stole me because you were afraid I'd get swept off my feet by someone else?"

"Rokan says so. He is never wrong." I clench my fists at the thought.

"And did he say when this would happen?" When I shake my head no, her smile grows broader. "So you stole me because I might in the future resonate to another man and it made you jealous?"

I glare at her. Why is she not taking this seriously?

Brooke leans in and pinches my cheeks. "Oh my god, that is so cuuuuute! Seriously, I could eat you up. Look at how jealous you are! I love it!"

"You like my misery?" I am astonished.

"Not your misery, silly. I like how jealous you are. No one's ever been so possessive over me in the past. I love it." She wiggles, pleased, and smiles down at me. "It makes me feel wanted. I don't believe that hocus pocus shit anyhow."

"Rokan is never wrong."

Her smile fades a little. "You're really upset over this. You think he's right?"

I put a hand to my chest, over my heart. I can still feel it racing from our last bout of mating. Or perhaps I am frightened of losing my mate so quickly now that I have found her. "His khui," I tell her. "It guides him."

"Hmm." She puts her hand over her teats, pressing between them. "Resonance, huh? Tell me what it would feel like again? Maybe if I recognize the signs we can head it off at the pass."

"I do not know. I have never experienced it." I scowl at her. "Must we speak of this?" I do not want to think about it—or losing her—any more than I have to. Just the thought makes my heart race in my chest like a fleeing dvisti.

She swats my chest. "Humor me. Tell me what it feels like. Tell me what you've heard."

The look she gives me is intense, so I nod and think how best to describe it. I have heard it discussed many a time through many different tribesmates, and they all speak of it in similar ways. "We say that the khui is singing, though I think your people refer to it as humming or purring. Your khui will wake up, and when your perfect mate is near and the time is right for you to make a kit, it will begin its song—"

"Low at first?" Brooke asks, rubbing the valley between her teats. "Kind of subtle? Like you're not sure it's there?"

I nod. "I have heard it described as such, yes. You will be over-come with an intense desire to mate."

"Mmm, so it makes you horny. Got it." She looks thoughtful.

"Your heart will pound. Race as if you have been running for a long time."

"Go on."

"You will feel intense need for your mate. It will not abate until you mate enough that a kit is created."

She continues to rub the valley between her teats. "Any other physical signs? Or just intense neediness?" Brooke sounds breathless, as if discussing this is arousing her.

My cock rises in response. Perhaps we will not be leaving this cave for travel on this day, after all. "I hear a male's seed will change."

"Change, hmm? The taste changes?" She looks intrigued. "Or something else?"

"It becomes thicker."

"Oh, more sperm? That makes sense." Brooke sounds breathless. She skims her hands over her teats and then down to cup her cunt. "Does the female get wetter? Does the singing of the khui make things feel better? Like vibratey better?"

"I do not know." I give her a curious look, trying to ignore the need surging through me to answer her questions seriously "Why?"

"No reason." She bites her lip and then slides a bit closer to me. "So if my cootie were purring, would it sound like this?" She takes my hand and places it between her teats, over her heart. "Or stronger?"

I frown, about to pull my hand away when I realize...she is humming. The song is faint, but I can feel it in her chest, low and steady. "You...you are resonating?" I am shocked.

"I think so." She gives a nervous, excited little laugh. "I thought I was just twitchy and on edge this morning. And horny. Really horny." Her voice changes to a breathless note. "I've been feeling it a little off and on since last night. Does it come on gradually?"

"I do not know. Most of the time it is fierce and immediate, like lightning."

"But maybe I'm just not ovulating totally yet," Brooke says, smiling at me. "It might get stronger over the next day or two, until my eggs are totally ready. Or something. I don't know how my physiology's going to work with a cootie changing things up."

I am lost, her words strange ones. "I do not follow. Off-yew…"

She waves a hand. "Doesn't matter." Her eyes are bright and happy, and she bursts out into laughter. "How are you so calm about this?"

Calm? I am shocked. Beyond shocked. Stunned. I do not understand how this is happening. "How are you resonating when there is no male around?" I get up and race to the front of the cave, staring out into the snow. Is someone approaching? But the day is clear, and no one is near our cave. The snows are fresh and unspoiled. Confused, I turn back to Brooke.

She erupts into giggles, then pats the furs. "Come sit."

I do, though my panic is starting to creep in. She is resonating, but it is slow. "Someone must be coming," I tell her, realization dawning. "He is coming for you, and when he arrives—"

Brooke shakes her head. "He who? What are you talking about?"

"Your mate!" My heart gives a frantic thump at the thought, and I have to fight the urge to pin her down and mount her like an animal, all to stake my claim. "We must leave here. Run away. We—"

She grabs my cock, silencing me. "Calm down," she says softly. "No one's coming."

I am so startled by her arousing touch that my brain momentarily fogs. I cannot think. The world does not exist beyond her fingers gripping my shaft. Then I realize what she is saying. "No, Brooke. Someone—"

"I'm resonating," she continues in that low, gentle voice, even as she strokes my already-hard shaft. Her fingers move up and down and she pumps me hard once, twice. "I'm surprised you haven't figured out that I'm resonating to you, silly."

"You...we..." I shake my head. "I would feel it. I would know it...wouldn't I?"

"Maybe you're so dazzled from our lovemaking that you haven't been paying attention." Her smile is beautiful to see. "Maybe it's as quiet as mine and you haven't noticed because you've been too focused on other things."

"Other...things," I repeat slowly, not entirely sure she is making sense.

"Yup." She pumps my cock again, and then to my shock, bends over and takes the head of it into her mouth. She suckles me like I have her teats, and I gasp, startled at the intense sensation.

"Brooke!" I tug at her shoulder. "Do not! I will come—"

She lifts her head, and her laughter is throaty and sweet and makes my sac tighten with need. "I'm conducting an experiment, silly. I want to make you come."

"You...you do?" My heart pounds so loud I cannot think clearly. Or is it resonance? I do not know.

"Yep. I want to see if it's thicker. If there's are more swimmers in your stuff." She glances down at my cock and then grins up at me. "I guess we have enough evidence right here, though."

I look down to see what she is so proud of. There, dotting the head of my cock, are several beads of seed. As I watch, another rolls down the head. That is nothing unusual...except...

I watch in wonder as she touches it and lifts the droplet onto her finger. "Thicker. Milkier. Man, I never thought I'd study a guy's spunk so closely." She licks her finger, and I shudder at how aroused that makes me. "Tastes the same, I'm afraid."

I grab her and pull her against me. "Brooke," I pant. "Does this mean—"

"I'm pretty sure," she says with a giggle.

I pull her against my chest, pressing her face to my front. "Tell me what you hear!"

She giggles again and then goes quiet, listening. "I hear you. It's faint, but I hear you." She sits up, beaming, and then pats her chest. "Come listen to mine."

I pull her against me and lean in, pressing my ear to her chest. She sputters as my horns get in her face, so I move a bit lower. My jaw is cradled against the swells of her teats, my ear pressed to her skin. I wait.

There...soft and pleasant, the thrumming, gentle sound of her khui. Resonance.

I laugh with pure joy.

My khui is not lazy, or wrong, or choosy. It was waiting for my Brooke all this time.

Her smile is beautiful to see, and I pull her against me. "Resonance," I whisper, and my voice is husky with emotion. "My Brooke and resonance together. My heart cannot hold so much."

"It's going to have to learn," she tells me playfully. "Because I spy with my little human eye, a man that should claim his mate right about now..."

26

BROOKE

$\mathscr{I}$ wake up the next morning to something that sounds like a distant lawnmower. When the rush of desire hits me—stronger and far more powerful than any alien roofie—I realize that resonance has kicked into full swing, and I wake Taushen up with my mouth.

We don't get up from the furs that day.

Or the next.

By day three, we're sufficiently wrung out and our cooties have taken on a less insistent hum to something more pleasant and sated. Thank god. I love sex, and I love sex with Taushen more than anything, but even I can get tired of mating after a while. We doze a lot on day three. Or at least, I do. Whenever I wake up, Taushen's stoking the fire, making me food, and then insisting I go back to bed and sleep. I do, but only if he joins me. I sleep better with him to curl up against.

We stay at the cave for another five days, all told. It takes a day or two of heavy hunting to refill the cache with what we've borrowed, and while Taushen lays traps, I gather dung chips and debris for replenishing the fuel supply for the cave. Once it's self-sufficient once more, we head out in the direction of the "great salt lake," as the sa-khui like to call it. Taushen says when he sees Rokan again, he doesn't know whether he's going to choke him or hug him. "He said you would resonate," he tells me for the dozenth time, wonder and annoyance in his voice. "And I did not think to ask about me!"

It's been almost a month since we've parted from the tribe, and Taushen and I discuss if we should actually head back to the village directly instead of heading to the ocean. What if the tribe isn't there any longer? What if we're weeks too late to rendezvous with them? But at the end of the day, I still want to see the ocean. If the tribe isn't there, we can consider this just extending our vacation, and I'll get to see a little bit more of this planet that's now mine and have a bit more alone time with this big, sexy male that's also now mine.

No complaints here.

It takes about a week of walking—interrupted by a lot of stops to make out—before the air starts to carry the faint scent of salt in it.

"We are close," Taushen tells me, despite the ominous cliffs and the fact that the mountains seem to be getting bigger the closer we get to the water. We take a long, winding route through the mountains, and I bundle up in my furs to fight off the cold wind that seems to be higher here.
On the other side of the mountains we climb the edge of a cliff, and I can see the ocean for miles and miles. I gasp at the sight of the green, jewel-like water. It's not blue like the Caribbean back home, but almost jade green, and dark. Everything's so dark, even the sand far below. Icebergs float slowly past, and the surface of

the water seems to be dotted with white and greenish-white ice. In the distance, there's something that looks like a tuft of smoke on the horizon—or a storm cloud.

There's no sign of a ship, though.

I turn to Taushen, worried. "Is this the right place?"

He nods. "We come here during the bitter season to get salt and fish. If they are still here, this is the spot they will be at." He gestures at a distant break in the cliffs. "We will cut through that valley down to the ground. There are caves there, and they will have supplies even if the others have come and gone already." He smiles at me and takes the small pack from my shoulders. "Do not worry, my Brooke. You are always safe with me."

"Mmm, you say that, but I saw those sky-claw yesterday, just as you did." I let him take my pack, and I double-check the knotted tether that holds us together. It's a bit awkward walking with a three-foot-long rope holding us together, but it's better than getting eaten by a big dinosaur-looking bird.

"Bah. They were not close."

"That doesn't make me feel any better," I tell him. "Because that means those damn things are even bigger."

"I told you they were big," he says with a playful grin, and as he takes the lead once more and guides us through the valley, I keep a hand on his belt and my gaze on the skies. He tells me all about the story of Josie and Haeden, and how Haeden saved his mate from being swallowed whole by a sky-claw. Josie's petite, but she's not *that* much smaller than me. Not the most comforting story to tell a gal when she's nervous, but his confidence is appealing. If he's not worried, I suppose I shouldn't be, either.

I don't tell him to shut up, though. I'm too pleased with his cheery attitude. I love how happy Taushen is lately. Gone are his scowls and moody stares. It's like he's become a whole new person, one ready to meet the day with eagerness and one who wants to conquer the world. I love that, just as much as I love waking up to his kisses, and I'll take all his stories and laughter and be glad for every bit of them.

We're not even halfway through the canyon when Taushen turns and studies me. "Time for rest."

"I'm fine," I reassure him. "I can keep going."

"You can, but we will rest anyhow." He takes my elbow with gentle hands and leads me to a nearby rock, the perfect size to sit down, and makes sure I'm settled before he sits next to me. He offers me his waterskin, and a bite to eat from his trail pouch.

I do my best not to roll my eyes at all the fussing. He's like a mother hen now that I'm carrying his kit. You'd think I was made of spun glass the way he treats me, and most of the time...okay, most of the time I eat that shit up. Sometimes I get a little tired of it, though. I'm perfectly healthy, and even though I'm not super excited about the thought of being pregnant for almost a year and a half, I'm growing more and more fond of the idea of a family.

Me. Him. Our baby.

I think of Taushen as a father, and I have to admit, my heart melts at the thought of him holding our baby. He's going to be such a good daddy. However kind and gentle he is with me, I can only imagine how amplified that will be when we have our son...or daughter. I think I'd like a daughter for him to spoil. It's early yet, of course. I don't feel different, other than my cootie purrs every time I get near him, and my breasts felt a little tender this morning when we were having sex. Other than that, it's business as usual. That's fine for me right now, because I'm not ready to have an enormous belly just yet. I'm still getting used to the whole "resonated" thing.

"You are smiling," he says, with a curious glance at me.

"Just thinking about you and our baby."

His beaming smile fills me with warmth, and when he reaches out to touch my flat stomach, I'm pretty sure that no woman's ever felt so special or loved.

After we've finished resting, we start walking again, and I'm pleased when the path slopes down and winds its way onto the sands.

"Holy cow," I breathe, as I get my first up-close glimpse of the ocean here. My memories of going to the beach on spring break with my friends are nothing like the reality here. The sand is dark, just like the water, and more of that strange, dark jade green that seems so surreal. My furry boots look like bright specks of lint against the dark sand, and I bend down to grab a handful. It feels like Earth sand, maybe a little coarser. Something loud crashes onto the shore, and I nearly fall on my butt in surprise.

"Just a wave," Taushen tells me, hooking his hands under my arms and hefting me back to my feet as if I weigh nothing. "Do not be alarmed. I have you, my mate."

I cast him a grateful smile, but I can't stop staring at the water. "Just" a wave, my ass. Like Godzilla is "just" a lizard. That wave was enormous, and as I watch, another greenish, frothing wave rolls up onto the shore and crashes with a boom against the jagged rocks at the water's edge. No gentle beach here. From ground level, I can't see the foggy storm that hung over the distance, nor can I see many of the glaciers that float in the stretch of water. I look in surprise as something moves near my foot and shriek when something spidery scuttles near my boot. I fling myself into Taushen's arms and am relieved when he holds me off the ground. "What the fuck is that?"

"A crawler," he says simply. "Har-loh and Rukh call them sand-scorpions."

"It's hideous." It looks like a crab and a monster mated and had a leggy baby.

"It is good eating. Are you hungry?"

"Fuuuuck no." I press my face against his neck, and shudder.

He strokes my back, chuckling. "They will not harm you, my mate. This I promise."

"Lies," I tell him flatly, but I let him put me back down again. I guess it'll look bad if he has to carry me like a princess across the sand to meet the others. I'm relieved when his fingers link with mine, though. Just holding his hand makes me feel better.

"There are many strange-looking things to eat here," he tells me as we pick our way across the sand. "I will make you a meal of them later."

"I can hardly wait," I say dryly. "So, where are the caves?"

"Around the bend," he explains, pointing at the rocky cliffs in the distance.

As if someone else can hear our conversation, a figure appears, walking alone on the beach. It's covered in thick furs, but the form is unmistakably human, and when the woman turns to the breeze, I see a distinct, bulging pregnant belly under her layers of clothing.

"It's Harlow," I tell Taushen, and wave my free hand excitedly at her. "They're here, after all. They haven't left." I glance around again. "I don't see the ship, though."

"Maybe they have already destroyed it." Taushen doesn't sound sad about it. I guess to him, it's just another threat.

We head forward, toward the edge of the water, to greet Harlow. I wave again, but when she doesn't wave back, I start to feel a little peculiar.

As we get closer, I realize that this woman isn't Harlow.

It's a completely different pregnant woman.

Mystified, I shoot a look at Taushen, then turn back to the woman we're approaching. Definitely not Harlow. She doesn't have the bright red hair or the delicate build. This woman has dark hair that's pulled into two braids, and a rounded face. She rubs a hand over her belly and gives us a wary look as we approach, as if she's ready to bolt.

"Hi," I call out, not sure what to think. "You're with the tribe, aren't you?"

She hesitates, glances behind her, and then nods. "You must be Taushen and Buh-brukh." Her gaze fixes on my fading pink hair.

"Er, yeah. You can call me Brooke."

A reluctant smile crosses her face. She's a few years older than me, but not much, and she's got the cutest gap between her front teeth. Her face is a good one, a friendly one. "Brooke? That sounds a bit more likely to me. I'm Angie." She puts a hand to her lower back and stretches a little. "It's nice to meet you."

"I'm sorry, I know it's rude to bring it up, but...you already resonated?" I can't help but ask, putting a hand to my own flat belly. "To who?"

The look on her face grows sad, and she pushes a stray strand of hair out of her face before glancing away. "No resonance. This one was with me when I woke up." And she rubs her belly again. "As for the father...I don't know who—or what—he was."

Oh no.

27

TAUSHEN

The human called An-shee does not speak much as she leads us across the beach. It is not as if I need a guide; I have been on these shores many times with my tribe. But she seems to feel it is her task, so I let her. My Brooke is disturbed by her pregnant belly and shoots me worried looks. I am less worried than she is. If An-shee does not have a mate to feed her and her kit, the tribe will help out. All kits are welcome amongst us and treasured by all.

As we approach, I see clusters of people on the beach itself. Cashol casts nets into the water, speaking with a pair of males that look strikingly similar to each other. Their skin has a ruddy cast to it, which makes the blue of their khui seem that much brighter in their faces. They have been awake for some time, then, if the tribe has hunted sa-kohtsk for them. Normally I would be sad to miss such an exciting hunt, but I was with my Brooke. Nothing can be better than that.

We pass Leezh teaching two strange human women to make fire. She looks up at us and nods, then slaps the hand of one girl when she reaches for a coal with bone tongs. "Don't touch that shit. What are you, five?"

The girl pulls her hand back and gives Leezh a wounded look. "Sorry."

"It's bone. All our utensils are bone. Bone burns. It took my ass twelve hours to carve that shit and I don't want you burning it."

Brooke opens her mouth to say something, but I tug on her hand and pull her along. There will be time enough to greet all the newcomers. First we must find our chief.

Near the mouth of one of the larger caves, Har-loh and Rukh sit with a cluster of females, helping them with their sewing. "You want to reinforce your seams, like Rukh is doing," Har-loh says, gesturing at her mate's sewing. "You don't want your leathers falling apart on you, because the reality of it is, you're not going to have that many changes of clothes. And any hole will make a really unpleasant breeze."

The females lean in, gazing at Rukh's stitches, and then one looks up at me. She elbows her friend, and then everyone is staring at Brooke and myself.

"Hi," Brooke says with another wave of her hand. "Uh, we're back."

"I'd get up to hug you but it'll take all day," Har-loh says, with a pat on her belly. Her face is wreathed in a happy smile. "I'm glad to see you two." Her smile at me is more uncertain, but when she realizes we are holding hands, her smile grows once more. "You've missed a lot."

"I can tell." Brooke squeezes my hand. "I'm just glad we ran into you guys again. I'm surprised everyone's still at the beach."

Har-loh's expression falters, and she exchanges a look with her mate.

"You should find chief," Rukh says to us, and touches Har-loh's knee possessively. "Much to talk about."

"That is where we are headed," I tell him. "Where can we find him?"

Rukh points inside the largest of caves, and I nod and all but drag Brooke behind me.

"Bye," Brooke calls out, trotting after me. "I'll be back later!"

The females giggle, and one says something under her breath that makes their laughter grow.

"So many new people," Brooke tells me, breathless. "It's going to take some getting used to. We're not the new ones anymore!"

"No male can claim you now," I say to her. "You belong to me."

"That's adorable that you're getting all caveman on me again." Brooke nudges me with her elbow. "Don't tell me you didn't see those girls checking you out."

"Checking...out? What were they checking?" I frown.

"Your butt, most likely." She pulls her hand from mine and pats my bottom. "It's a really nice one."

I can feel my face grow hot. "Well, I am yours. They can look all they want, but I belong to you."

"My thoughts exactly," she says with a happy sigh, and I notice she keeps her hand on my bottom even as we walk. I guess I am not the only one that feels possessive, and the thought pleases me greatly.

Vektal is inside the largest cave, surrounded by baskets of

supplies. He sits with another human, this one rounded like Mah-dee but with dark hair. She has a rock that she scratches on, and shakes her head at Vektal when he puts a fur into one pile. "You can't put that there," she tells him. "I've already counted those. It goes in the other stack. I..." She pauses, blinking at us. "We have visitors."

"Eh?" My chief turns, and then a look of relief crosses his face at the sight of us. "Finally you show your faces."

Brooke squeezes my hand, showing me support.

"We have returned," I say boldly. "Brooke is my mate."

"I would hear this from Buh-brukh's lips," Vektal says, crossing his arms over his chest.

"It's true. We even resonated," she tells him, and pats her stomach. "Bun in the oven and everything."

"Resonance, hmm?" Vektal rubs his chin and then gives me a look. "Rokan told me of what he confessed to you. That Buh-brukh was to resonate soon, and that was why you stole her. I have to admit, I am not pleased."

My breath catches in my throat. I sense exile is coming on, and the thought makes my heart hurt. I will lose my friends, my home, everything. But when Brooke touches my arm, I straighten. I am not afraid of whatever punishment he doles out. It will be worth it. Brooke is everything to me. I would risk exile a thousand times to have her at my side. "I understand you are angry, but I would do the same thing all over again. For Brooke, I will risk everything. She is my mate in all ways, and if you must exile me, do so."

The chief snorts, shaking his head slowly. "I have learned over these seasons that punishing for such things is impossible. It does not stop the actions, and as long as the female is happy, I see no reason to make matters worse." He gives us a stern look. "Do not think that you are getting away easily simply because my mate is not here."

"We would never think such a thing," Brooke tells him, and I recognize she is using her sweet voice on him, the persuasive one. She holds my arm and leans in against me, looking soft and fragile. "And we can't thank you enough for being understanding."

"It is less understanding and more that I have bigger problems," Vektal admits, glancing down at the female at his feet. "A happy resonance is the least of my worries."

"You ain't lyin'," the female says with a shake of her head.

Vektal frowns at her, as if displeased with her agreement, but the female does not seem to notice. She takes the fur he has placed in the pile, moves it to another pile, and then makes a mark on her rock again.

"What is it?" I ask, curious. "Did something go wrong with the ship?" The humans we passed seemed content enough, and they were taking lessons from the tribe. I did not see fighting or anger, only surprise that we had arrived.

"Oh no, he burned our only chance of escape and then sank it. He did that just *fine*," the mouthy, round female says and makes another mark on her rock. Her words sound bitter and playful all at once.

My chief rolls his eyes at the female. I suspect he has heard this argument before. "Ha-nah, take Buh-brukh out and introduce her to the new members of our tribe. I must speak with Taushen privately."

The human—Ha-nah—gets to her feet. "Come on, you get to meet our fun crew. We're a total party and a half, wait and see." Her tone is dry and odd.

Brooke's mouth twitches with amusement, and she pulls me down and gives me a kiss on the cheek. "Be good," she whispers, and then pats my bottom one more time before turning to leave with the female.

I flick her bottom with my tail, and she squeals with laughter, holding her backside before she trots away. I do not miss the human female rolling her eyes, but I do not care. I am happy with my Brooke, and she is happy with me. I do not care what anyone else thinks.

Vektal watches them go, a tired expression on his face. "That one is like Leezh, but without the charm," he comments.

"Leezh has charm?"

The chief grunts. "Ha-nah is like many of the others—they are not happy the ship was destroyed. They think they could fly themselves back to their planet, even though none of them know where it is or how to fly a spaceship." He rubs his brow. "Even Har-loh says they are like herding snowcats. They do not listen well, they are helpless, and they make me wish I was at home, tucked into the furs with my mate and my kits sleeping nearby. It has been far too long since I have seen their faces."

I nod agreement, watching out of the corner of my eye as my mate and the other female stop to talk to a male, one with strange, mottled golden skin. He smiles and laughs at them, and I have to fight the possessive surge in my belly. Brooke is mine. She has resonated to me. Let that male laugh and flirt with her all he wants. Her heart belongs to Taushen. I turn back to my chief. "So...no exile?"

Vektal just flicks his hands, dismissing the idea. "There is far too much going on to think about that right now. I will tell my Georgie that Buh-brukh was happy to go with you. There is nothing to punish if that is the case. We have different problems to figure out. I need every hunter right now."

"You said as much. What is going on?"

"Bek, Rokan, Zolaya, and Raahosh are out searching. One of the males was...not right in the head, and we have no healer. He has been crazed ever since we gave him a khui, something I now regret." Vektal's mouth thins and he looks frustrated. "We had to keep him tied so he would not hurt himself or anyone else, but one night he stole away...and took a female with him. It was not mutual. This female was shy, easily frightened. She would not have gone with him on her own."

"Resonance, perhaps?"

"Unlikely. Ashtar—that is the gold male—resonated to a human female named Vuh-ron-ca. No one else resonated. If the two missing ones resonated, then it did not happen while they were at camp." He shakes his head again. "And there were signs of a struggle. We are not sure that the male and female will know how to take care of themselves, so the others are searching for them. And they are not the only ones we are missing."

I am surprised. "There are more that have disappeared?"

His expression looks bleak. "Two more, and I fear this is my fault."

I hate to see him so unhappy, so uncertain of himself. This is not the chief I know. I have always looked up to him, first as an older hunter, and then when he took the mantle of leadership after his father died. Vektal has always been sure of his place in our tribe, sure of himself, sure of everything. To see him like this makes me see him as...like the rest of us. A regular hunter with problems, as I am. We are one and the same. "Tell me what happened. Perhaps I can help."

Vektal begins to pace. "It was the ship. Mardok and Har-loh were unhappy with the thought of destroying it, and I was focused on them and not paying attention to all my humans. We set it on fire and it floated for a time in the waters, steaming and hissing. It took many long hours for it to sink, and when it finally did, that is when we realized we were missing two of the human females— Lo-ren and Mar-ee-sol. We could not find them anywhere. We looked, and their packs were still here at camp, so they could not have left into the wild without them. They were just...gone. I realized after a time that we did not check to see if they were out of the ship before we set it on fire and rolled it down the beach and into the waters." He scrubs his face. "Foolish of me. I should have known. Mar-ee-sol likes to hide because she is frightened of everything. But I did not think, and there was so much going on..." He sighs heavily. "They are my responsibility, and I am failing them."

He speaks as if they are still alive and not dead with the ship under the waves. "Then...they live? You have seen them?"

"No. There is more to the story. Two days later, Mardok came to me and said he and Har-loh had hidden some of the ship's equipment away, just in case we needed it. They assured me that the enemy would not be able to find us with what they kept. I was not happy to hear this, but Mardok tells me that he gets readings of two humans, very far across the water."

I blink, surprised. "Across the water? Are they...floating on something?"

"Mardok thinks there is an island behind the fog. I think he has been talking to Jo-see too much." Vektal's smile is wry. "The fog never lifts, so there is no way of knowing, and Mardok says his readings are not always correct. That they disappear and appear again over and over. He does not know if the equipment is broken or if they are truly alive. He and Farli go up and down the beach every day, trying to get a better reading." He sighs heavily. "So until we find out if they are alive or dead, we wait. Until the feral one brings back the missing female—or the others find them— we wait." He clenches his jaw and shoots me a frustrated look. "And I stay here, away from my mate, who carries our kit, and my daughters, who I miss more than I thought possible."

I clasp a hand on his shoulder. Missing a mate, I understand. Brooke has only been gone from my side for the space of a few breaths and already I long for her return. I cannot imagine being apart from her for a full turn of the moon. "We will find them. We will not give up. Tell me what Brooke and I can do to help."

BROOKE

The vibe at camp is totally different with the new humans. There are sixteen newcomers, all told. Three guys and thirteen chicks, and Hannah is quick to tell me all about how the others went missing. "That's probably what they're talking about," she tells me matter-of-factly. "Vektal won't shut up about it."

"Do you hang out with Vektal a lot?" I ask, curious, as we head toward the group Harlow's teaching. The chief didn't seem to appreciate her presence much.

"Oh, I'm his assistant." She gives me a nod, as if that explains it all. "The man's clearly overwhelmed, so I appointed myself his helper. He'll thank me for it someday."

I'll bet. I bite back my chuckle, because Hannah seems nice enough, if a bit bossy. She's short and round, with brown pigtails and dimpled cheeks, like she's just stepped off of Gilligan's Island and into, well, Gilligan's Iceberg. I wouldn't say she's a cheerful sort like Mary-Ann from the show, though. She's definitely more of a grump, or, as Liz refers to her, the "salty daughter I never had." Doesn't surprise me that the two of them get along.

We wind through the camp, stopping to talk to everyone. Names and faces blur together, but I try to remember most of them. Ashtar is the big, friendly guy with golden, scaly skin and whirling eyes that change colors despite his khui. He's sweet enough, if a bit strange-looking—and this is coming from a girl who just mated a big, blue, horned dude. He dotes on Veronica, who seems like his polar opposite. She's plain, soft-spoken, and completely average-looking, but above average in klutziness. If someone's burned their fingers on the fire or spilled dinner, it's Veronica. If someone needs to be rescued from the tide before it washes her away, it's Veronica. If someone's going to find sand-scorpions in her bed at night, it's Veronica. I kind of feel sorry for her, and I haven't said more than two words to her. She sounds unlucky as hell. She also doesn't seem to realize how much Ashtar likes her, because she seems shy and uncertain around him. They'll figure it out, I'm sure.

The other two new guys back at camp are twins. I don't remember their names, nor do I remember them saying much when Hannah introduced us. They stare, intensely blue eyes narrowed, as if they're sizing me up to either kill me or kiss me. I sincerely hope neither one happens, and I make sure to point out that my mate's talking with the chief. They don't look friendly. Hannah says they were gladiators of some kind. I think it'll take me a while to get used to them. A long, long while.

Then there's pregnant Angie, who seems to keep to herself. A lean, sweet-faced blonde named Raven (of all things). Chatty Devi, who used to be a scientist and now seems intent on talking Liz's ear off. There's Tia, who looks to be no more than sixteen, and Nadine, who's got the most glorious, natural, kinky curls (I'm a hair stylist, I notice hair). There's Steph, who's redheaded like Harlow, but not freckled. A brunette. A Hispanic girl and a Filipina. A blonde. After a while, I hit saturation point and just nod, giving up on names. There'll be time to learn everyone's faces later.

They're not going anywhere.

As the day wears on, more people trickle back into camp. Farli and Mardok return and give me hugs, and I even pet Farli's goofy-looking Chompy, who slobbers all over my hands with happiness and then tries to eat my sleeve. "He likes the taste of leather best when it is worn by someone who resonates," Farli tells me with a teasing grin.

"I'm going to say ew to that," I reply, because I can only imagine what the hell Chompy smells on my leathers. Laundry day tomorrow, for sure.

She only laughs, pleased. "I have gone through more leathers in the last two turns of the moon than I have in many seasons. Hide your leggings when you sleep at night."

It takes me a moment to realize that she knows we've resonated. I haven't exactly been blasting it around the camp—except to the two intense-looking twins—because I don't know how Taushen wants to tell everyone. Do we make a big announcement? Act cool about it? What? "How'd you guess?"

"Guess?" She laughs, a smile crossing her pretty blue face. "There is no guessing. I can hear you."

I put a hand to my breast, and sure enough, I'm humming. It gets louder and louder, and a moment later, a big arm encircles my shoulders and Taushen pulls me against him, nuzzling my messy, tangled hair. "My mate," he murmurs against my skin. "I have missed you."

I feel myself blushing.

"Leggings," Farli advises. "Hide them well."

"Keep your ugly pony away from my shorts," I tease her back as she walks away.

Taushen nips my ear, sending shivers through me. "We will have a private cave tonight, Vektal assures me. He understands well how demanding resonance can be and does not wish for us to wake the others."

Oh, jeez.

Hannah wrinkles her nose at us. "Uh, yeah, I'm going to go and see if Liz needs help with the fire-making. Or something. You two keep making out. Don't mind me." She hurries away.

I just laugh. "I think we've become those people, Taushen. We're PDA jerks."

"What is pee-dee-ayy?" He licks the shell of my ear. "And why does that make us jerks?"

"Public displays of affection," I explain to him, though it's hard to concentrate when he's nipping at my ear like that. "And it makes us jerks because we're showing off."

"I do not care if the world knows that you are my mate. Let them see how proud I am of you."

He's lucky he's holding on to me, because my knees get weak at his words.

28

BROOKE

*A*s the sun goes down, the fire's built higher and higher until we have a bonfire going. It surprises me to see such a big fire, because most fires the sa-khui make tend to be small and designed only to give a bit of heat and light. Since they run off of dung, that's a lot of dung, but here on the beach, we're burning wood and it reminds me starkly of home and bonfires back on the beach when I was a teenager.

"There's a lot of driftwood," Harlow explains to me as we sit near the fire. Both Rukh and Taushen stand close to it, skewers in hand, and quietly chat with Salukh and Pashov, who are showing the others how to roast their own food. "The fire comforts the newcomers. They feel safer with a familiar fire, and there's so much driftwood that washes up that we started pulling it in from the tide and airing it in the sunlight."

"But where's all the driftwood coming from?" I ask her, bewildered. I think of all the trees I've seen in the past, the flippy, sticky, pink ones that cover the valleys, and the wispy blue ones higher in the mountains. These logs are enormous and thick, like trees back on Earth. "Not that I'm complaining. It's just weird to see."

"Who knows," Harlow says with a shrug. Angie comes and sits down next to her, and Harlow beams a smile in her direction, her attention diverted. "How are you doing?"

Angie's smile is soft, shy. "Hanging in there."

"Hungry?" I see the motherly aspects of Harlow starting to take over, judging from the protective smile on her face as she watches Angie. I guess someone has to look out for the poor pregnant lady. "I'll get Rukh to cook enough for you, too," she says, and reaches out to lightly touch her mate's arm.

"I shall feed you, An-shee. It will be my honor." One of the reddish twins steps forward, his hard face impassive. He carries a thick slab of bloody meat and holds it out to her. "Does this meet your approval?"

"Oh. Uh." Angie blinks and looks at me and Harlow, uncertain.

"I think Angie probably prefers her meat cooked, big guy," I tell him helpfully. "Pregnancy belly and all that."

The red guy stares down at the meat in his hands, and then back at Angie. "Then this does not meet your approval."

She bites her lip. "I, um, things stay down better when they're cooked."

He bows at her. "I will correct this shameful mistake." With that, he takes the meat and retreats to the far side of the fire, leaning in close to speak to his brother. There's a scowl on his face.

Angie looks worried. "Did I do something wrong?" she whispers.

"I'm sure it's fine," I tell her breezily. "He can suck it up. You don't offer pregnant ladies raw meat, even on Earth. And Taushen can cook for you if your friend's too pissy to cook, right, babe?" I reach out and stroke Taushen's tail.

My mate stiffens, back going ramrod straight. It's like I just grabbed his dick in front of everyone, and he shoots me a wide-eyed stare. Whoops. "Is my food ready?" I say brightly, hoping that no one notices in the firelight that I'm blushing. Harlow's discreetly looking away, and Salukh clears his throat—or maybe he's laughing. It's hard to tell.

"I will feed you," Taushen replies in a choked voice, and I notice my cootie's rather loud, which means his is, too. Whoops again. I resist the urge to cross my arms over my now-pricking nipples.

"So what do you guys call this place?" Devi asks from across the fire, taking a big bite of raw meat and letting it gush down her chin.

"Well, some of us are Star Wars nerds," Liz says proudly. "So—"

"More like just you," Harlow retorts. "No one else knows this stuff but you."

She shrugs, pleased. "Least I didn't name my kid Jar Jar. Or Dooku. Anyhow, we call this place Not-Hoth because it's like the snow planet in that movie, but not."

Devi's brows draw together and she frowns. "Oh, you can't call it that."

"Why not?" I ask, curious.

"It needs its own name. If I discovered a new species of butterfly, for example, I couldn't call it Not-Monarch. It'd be something entirely different and it deserves its own moniker." She shrugs her shoulders. "Otherwise we just go around calling everyone not-humans or we're eating not-chicken."

"We do that anyhow," I point out, thinking of not-potatoes.

"Doesn't seem right," another girl chimes in. "We need a real name."

"What would you call it?" Vektal asks, moving to stand near the fire. He watches everyone with weary eyes, and it looks to me like he's more than ready to go home. Poor guy. I bet he misses Georgie something fierce.

"Hell," Hannah mutters. "Frozen over."

A few people chuckle.

Devi ignores that. "Something all its own. I don't know. I'm not good with names." She spreads her hands and then stares at them. Then she licks her fingers surreptitiously and grins at her neighbor.

"Something that talks about a fresh start, maybe," another girl chimes in.

"Two Suns?" another adds. Steph, I think.

"Home?" someone else quips.

"Icehome," Angie says in a soft voice.

"Oh, I like that." Harlow smiles. "Same, but different."

"I like Icehome, too," another person chimes in.

"I like Not-Hoth," Liz says with a shrug. "You say potato, I say not-potato."

"It can be Icehome to us," the young girl—Tia—says.

"It can be Icehome for everyone," Vektal agrees, nodding with approval. "As long as it is home."

"Well, it's not like we have any other options," Nadine replies, laughing. A few others chuckle. Some—like Hannah—don't. It's going to take time for everyone to adjust.

Heck, they have all the time in the world.

"To Icehome," Devi says, raising a chunk of raw meat into the air.

"Ew, gross, are you seriously going to eat that?" Tia squeals.

"Why not?" Devi says with a shrug. "When in Rome and all that."

"To Icehome," I say, raising my waterskin into the air. I like the thought.

"Icehome," Taushen replies, glancing back at me. His eyes are warm, and I feel my khui beginning to purr a little harder. Oh boy. I suddenly want to grab his tail again.

I suddenly want to grab more than his tail.

I must show it on my face, because Taushen turns toward me, stepping away from the fire. He kneels in front of me and offers me the skewer of barely cooked meat. "Hungry?" His voice is husky and low and oh-so-delicious.

I grab a hunk off the top and shove it into my mouth, not caring that it's so raw it's practically twitching. I chew fast, swallow quickly, and then eat another hunk while Taushen watches me with hungry, hungry eyes.

"Wow, you must be starving," Harlow comments.

"Totally," I manage between bites. "Sooo hungry." I eat as fast as I can, and when my skewer's empty, I jump to my feet. "I sure am beat now, though."

Liz snorts, her eyebrows going up. "Ain't gonna be the only thing getting beat tonight, if you know what I'm saying."

Someone giggles.

I don't even care. "See you guys in the morning." I'm not even going to fake a yawn. I just grab my mate by his belt and give him a meaningful look. "Ready to go to bed?"

"More than ready." He grabs me and, to my surprise, hauls me into his arms and then over his shoulder like a sack of potatoes. His hand goes possessively to my butt, and he nods at the others. "I must take my mate away now."

Laughter and a few waves send us off. I could swear Vektal's lips are twitching with amusement as we leave the fire, but I have to admit I'm not paying all that much attention. I'm far more fascinated by the hand on my butt.

We leave behind the light of the fire and the low murmurs of conversation, and it's quieter the closer we get to the water. "Our cave is set up this way," Taushen explains, and I could swear the man's practically racing across the sand. His steps are hurried, as if he's just as eager as I am.

"Mmm, sounds good to me." I wonder if I can undo the laces on my tunic while he walks.

We make it to the cave a short walk later, and then Taushen sets me down inside, ever so gently, on my feet. "Wait here and I will make you a fire," he tells me, and then cups my face and gives me a quick kiss.

"Fuck the fire," I breathe, grabbing at his tunic. "We've got furs, right? Good enough for me."

He groans, and then we're ripping at each other's clothing, desperate to feel skin. I manage to pull his tunic over his head and get his pants down around his knees before he figures out my clothing, but that's okay. I help him pull the rest of it off of me, and then we both fall into the furs, together. Our mouths are frantic, our kisses heated, and I push him onto his back.

"Let me," I whisper, and slide a leg over his chest.

I love the way he sucks in his breath and goes still underneath me, like he doesn't know what's going to come next, but it's going to be glorious. I love that about him. I love his sweet, innocent side, as well as the dirty, hair-pulling side. I love how protective and caring he is. I love how good he makes me feel. I love his smiles.

I take Taushen's cock in my hand and guide him to my core, skipping foreplay entirely. I don't need it, I'm wet with need and my cootie's going a mile a minute, singing to his like there's no tomorrow. The breath hisses between his teeth as I sink down onto him, and I can't stop the moan that breaks from my throat. Like this, he feels so very deep inside me, and when I sink down just right, I can rub his spur against my clit in the best of ways... "We might have to do this more often," I tell him with a gasp, rising up and then sliding down onto him again.

"Anything you want, my mate. I am yours." His words are fervent, breathless.

I guide his big hands to my waist and as he holds on to me, I ride him. I'm not the most gentle, but he doesn't seem to care. One big hand leaves my waist and plays with my breasts while I keep a steady, rolling rhythm with my hips. It feels so good, so powerful to move on top of him like this, and I feel like the sexiest woman in the world.

I come with a shudder, and he grabs my waist and plunges into me, raising his hips to meet mine, and then he's coming, too, his body rigid under mine, my name on his lips. I caress his face, whispering his name while he releases. I love this moment, the sheer bliss in his face even as his expression contorts with the force of his orgasm. I slide down onto him as he relaxes, and his spur jabs me in an overly sensitive place, so I roll off of him.

He immediately pulls me against him, not caring that we're a little sticky and sweaty from our heated lovemaking. "My mate," he says, pressing a kiss to my shoulder. "Is this your home?"

It seems a strange thing to ask, but then I remember the conversations about Icehome, and Hannah's unhappy look. "For a while, I wasn't sure," I admit honestly. "I cried a lot when we first got here. I was scared, and then I didn't like the thought of being stranded. But I'm coming around."

"What has changed your mind?" He nuzzles my throat.

I chuckle. Fishing for compliments. That's cute. "Humans have a saying, you know. Home is where the heart is. I thought it was just silly nonsense until I met you. I love everything about you, Taushen, and I'm glad I'm here with you. Icehome really does feel like a home now. My home, because my heart is here."

I feel him nod against me, his face buried against my neck. "Even though I was born here, I feel I did not have a place until you kissed me."

I wrap my arms around this sweet, beautiful, strong man. "Then I'm glad I'm here to bring you home."

AUTHOR'S NOTE

Hi again!

Right now you're probably feeling one of two ways. You're ready to murder me right now for adding sixteen new girls, or you're excited for the addition of sixteen new girls and are ready to murder me because there's so much story to be uncovered.

So.

Much.

Story.

To be honest, this has all been boiling in my head for a while. I wasn't sure how to bring it all around, but I knew it was a direction I wanted things to go in. Of course, the longer you sit on something, the more it begins to take shape in your head, and eventually when it's ready to be a book, it pops out, fully grown, like Athena springing from Zeus' head in Greek Mythology. That's kind of how things are going with this series. I keep getting ideas for books and I can't write them all fast enough!

Terrible problem, I know. You'll just have to bear with me.

In the meantime, I wanted to let you guys know which direction things are heading.

IS THE ICE PLANET BARBARIANS SERIES OVER RUBY OMG HOW COULD YOU?

No. It is not over. Far from it! I just now got a story in my head for poor Ariana and she deserves her story. We still have Gail and Sessah (well, when he grows up a bit more) and Marlene and all the kits and even more stuff going on with the tribe that we've already met and yeah...they're not going anywhere.

HOWEVER.

The new people will have their own series. Instead of being Ice Planet Barbarians, it will be called The Icehome Series (or just Icehome) and the first book will star poor unfortunate Lauren, who disappeared in this book along with Marisol. Now where could they possibly be? Hmm. Hmm...

Hmm...

The new series will be completely stand alone. I want people to be able to pick it up even if they've fallen behind on IPB. Like PRISON PLANET BARBARIAN, there will be callbacks to the main series, but it'll be independent. So if you do not like the addition of the new people, you don't have to read them! I'm trying to make it easy for everyone, but of course I hope you'll read them. I have some exciting stuff planned for these ladies (and gents) and they'll be interacting with our little tribe quite a bit. Expect a ton of cameos from our favorite couples, of course. Someone's got to teach these poor kits how to survive on a darn ice planet.

You're probably wondering how this works with my schedule. Me too, to be honest! I think we'll bounce between the three on a regular basis. Next up in August is FIRE IN HIS EMBRACE –

Emma's book, book 3 of Fireblood Dragons. After that, we'll head over to ICEHOME #1, which will have some super swanky title I will think of at some point. Lauren's book. After that, it'll probably be Ariana's book (Ice Planet Barbarians #17) and then we'll swing back to more dragons.

Of course, this schedule is due to change, because right now I'm sitting (mentally) on Kivian's story (Remember him? Jutari's brother?) and it'll be out at some point. And I might have a slice of life story or two tucked away somewhere in there. And then I've got to work on a NY novel, and then there's this shiny, pretty project I've also been quietly sitting on because I haven't had time to write it yet.

(You'll get your turn, precious book, I promise).

Long story short, the barbarians aren't going anywhere. Please don't worry!

In the meantime, I just want to say thank you all for being such amazing fans. I wake up every day excited to write my crazy books because I know you guys will love it as much as I do. That's such a wonderful feeling. I cannot thank you guys enough for the enthusiasm and love you show me on a regular basis.

And speaking of love and enthusiasm, THANK YOU to Lydia Carr, who came up with the title. It's perfect, as you said, because Brooke's a bit of a tease and because she does hair. How can I not use that title, right?

All the love,

<3 Ruby

TRIBAL WHO'S WHO

As of the end of Barbarian's Tease (8 years post-human arrival)

Mated Couples and their kits

=======

Vektal (Vehk-tall) – The chief of the sa-khui. Mated to Georgie.

Georgie – Human woman (and unofficial leader of the human females). Has taken on a dual-leadership role with her mate. Currently pregnant with her third kit.

Talie (Tah-lee) – Their first daughter.

Vekka (Veh-kah) – Their second daughter.

=======

Maylak (May-lack) – Tribe healer. Mated to Kashrem.

Kashrem (Cash-rehm) - Her mate, also a leather-worker.

Esha (Esh-uh) – Their teenage daughter.

Makash (Muh-cash) — Their younger son.

=====

Sevvah (Sev-uh) – Tribe elder, mother to Aehako, Rokan, and Sessah

Oshen (Aw-shen) – Tribe elder, her mate

Sessah (Ses-uh) - Their youngest son

=====

Ereven (Air-uh-ven) Hunter, mated to Claire

Claire – Mated to Ereven

Erevair (Air-uh-vair) - Their first child, a son

Relvi (Rell-vee) – Their second child, a daughter

=====

Liz – Raahosh's mate and huntress.

Raahosh (Rah-hosh) – Her mate. A hunter and brother to Rukh.

Raashel (Rah-shel) – Their daughter.

Aayla (Ay-lah) – Their second daughter

=====

Stacy – Mated to Pashov. Unofficial tribe cook.

Pashov (Pah-showv) – son of Kemli and Borran, brother to Farli, Zennek, and Salukh. Mate of Stacy.

Pacy (Pay-see) – Their first son.

Tash (Tash) – Their second son.

=====

Nora – Mate to Dagesh. Currently pregnant after a second resonance.

Dagesh (Dah-zhesh) (the g sound is swallowed) – Her mate. A hunter.

Anna & Elsa – Their twin daughters.

———

Harlow – Mate to Rukh. Once 'mechanic' to the Elders' Cave. Currently pregnant after a second resonance.

Rukh (Rookh) – Former exile and loner. Original name Maarukh. (Mah-rookh). Brother to Raahosh. Mate to Harlow. Father to Rukhar.

Rukhar (Roo-car) – Their son.

———

Megan – Mate to Cashol. Mother to Holvek.

Cashol (Cash-awl) – Mate to Megan. Hunter. Father to Holvek.

Holvek (Haul-vehk) – their son.

———

Marlene (Mar-lenn) – Human mate to Zennek. French.

Zennek (Zehn-eck) – Mate to Marlene. Father to Zalene. Brother to Pashov, Salukh, and Farli.

Zalene (Zah-lenn) – daughter to Marlene and Zennek.

———

Ariana – Human female. Mate to Zolaya. Currently pregnant. Basic school 'teacher' to tribal kits.

Zolaya (Zoh-lay-uh) – Hunter and mate to Ariana. Father to Analay.

Analay (Ah-nuh-lay) – Their son.

=====

Tiffany – Human female. Mated to Salukh. Tribal botanist.

Salukh (Sah-luke) – Hunter. Son of Kemli and Borran, brother to Farli, Zennek, and Pashov.

Lukti (Lookh-tee) – Their son.

=====

Aehako (Eye-ha-koh) –Mate to Kira, father to Kae. Son of Sevvah and Oshen, brother to Rokan and Sessah.

Kira – Human woman, mate to Aehako, mother of Kae. Was the first to be abducted by aliens and wore an ear-translator for a long time.

Kae (Ki –rhymes with 'fly') – Their daughter.

=====

Kemli (Kemm-lee) – Female elder, mother to Salukh, Pashov, Zennek, and Farli. Tribe herbalist.

Borran (Bore-awn) – Her mate, elder. Tribe brewer.

=====

Josie – Human woman. Mated to Haeden. Currently pregnant for a third time.

Haeden (Hi-den) – Hunter. Previously resonated to Zalah, but she died (along with his khui) in the khui-sickness before resonance could be completed. Now mated to Josie.

Joden (Joe-den) – Their first child, a son.

Joha (Joe-hah) – Their second child, a daughter.

Rokan (Row-can) – Oldest son to Sevvah and Oshen. Brother to Aehako and Sessah. Adult male hunter. Now mated to Lila. Has 'sixth' sense.

Lila – Maddie's sister. Once hearing impaired, recently reacquired on *The Tranquil Lady* via med bay. Resonated to Rokan. Currently pregnant for a second time.

Rollan (Row-lun) – Their first child, a son.

Hassen (Hass-en) – Hunter. Previously exiled. Mated to Maddie.

Maddie – Lila's sister. Found in second crash. Mated to Hassen.

Masan (Mah-senn) – Their son.

Asha (Ah-shuh) – Mate to Hemalo. Mother to Hashala (deceased) and Shema.

Hemalo (Hee-muh-low) – Mate to Asha. Father to Hashala (deceased) and Shema.

Shema (Shee-muh) – Their daughter.

Farli – (Far-lee) Adult daughter to Kemli and Borran. Her brothers are Salukh, Zennek, and Pashov. She has a pet dvisti named Chompy (Chahm-pee). Mated to Mardok. Pregnant.

Mardok (Marr-dock) – Bron Mardok Vendasi, from the planet

Ubeduc VII. Arrived on *The Tranquil Lady*. Mechanic and ex-soldier. Resonated to Farli and elected to stay behind with the tribe.

═══

Bek – (Behk) – Hunter. Brother to Maylak. Mated to Elly.

Elly – Former human slave. Kidnapped at a very young age and has spent much of life in a cage or enslaved. First to resonate amongst the former slaves brought to Not-Hoth. Mated to Bek. Pregnant.

═══

Harrec (Hair-ek) – Hunter. Squeamish. Also a tease. Recently resonated to Kate.

Kate – Human female. Extremely tall & strong, with white-blonde curly hair. Recently resonated to Harrec. Pregnant.

═══

Warrek (War-ehk) – Tribal hunter and teacher. Son to Eklan (now deceased). Resonated to Summer.

Summer – Human female. Tends to ramble in speech when nervous. Chess aficionado. Recently resonated to Warrek.

═══

Taushen (Tow – rhymes with cow – shen) – Hunter. Recently mated to Brooke. Experiencing a happiness renaissance.

Brooke – Human female with fading pink hair. Former hair-dresser, fond of braiding the hair of anyone that walks close enough. Mated to Taushen and recently pregnant.

Unmated Elders

—————

Drayan (Dry-ann) – Elder.

Drenol (Dree-nowl) – Elder.

Vadren (Vaw-dren) – Elder.

Vaza (Vaw-zhuh) – Widower and elder. Loves to creep on the ladies. Currently flirting with Gail.

Former Unmated Human Slaves

—————

Gail – Divorced older human woman. Had a son back on Earth (deceased). Approx fiftyish in age. Allows Vaza to creep on her (she likes the attention). From the batch of 'Bek Rescues'.

Lauren – Pod girl. Went missing when the ship went down.

Marisol – Cowardly pod girl. Went missing when the ship went down.

Angie – Pregnant. Pod girl. Doesn't know who her baby daddy is.

Ashtar – Golden-skinned male slave, resonated to Veronica upon receiving khui.

Veronica – Clumsy human female who resonated to Ashtar upon receiving khui.

Hannah – Mouthy human pod girl. Set herself up as Vektal's assistant.

Tia – Youngest of pod girls.

Devi – Chatty scientist pod girl.

Steph

Nadine

Raven

Unnamed Red Twins

Unnamed other pod people (this will be filled in as we meet them!)

ICE PLANET BARBARIANS READING LIST

Are you all caught up on Ice Planet Barbarians? Need a refresher?
Click through to borrow or buy!

Ice Planet Barbarians – Georgie's Story
Barbarian Alien – Liz's Story
Barbarian Lover – Kira's Story
Barbarian Mine – Harlow's Story
Ice Planet Holiday – Claire's Story (novella)
Barbarian's Prize – Tiffany's Story
Barbarian's Mate – Josie's Story
Having the Barbarian's Baby – Megan's Story (short story)
Ice Ice Babies – Nora's Story (short story)
Barbarian's Touch – Lila's Story
Calm - Maylak's Story (short story)
Barbarian's Taming – Maddie's Story
Aftershocks (short story)
Barbarian's Heart – Stacy's Story
Barbarian's Hope – Asha's Story
Barbarian's Choice – Farli's Story
Barbarian's Redemption – Elly's Story

DRAGONS - NOW IN AUDIO!

Fire In His Blood is now in Audio! If you like listening to your books, won't you give it a try?

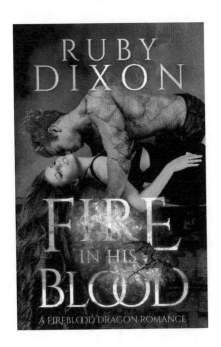

WANT MORE?

For more information about upcoming books in the Ice Planet Barbarians, Fireblood Dragons, or any other books by Ruby Dixon, like me on Facebook or subscribe to my new release newsletter. I love sharing snippets of books in progress and fan art! Come join the fun.

As always - thanks for reading!

<3 Ruby

PS - Want to discuss my books without me staring over your shoulder? There's a group for that, too! Ruby Dixon - Blue Barbarian Babes (over on Facebook) has all of your barbarian and dragon needs. :) Enjoy!

Made in the USA
Middletown, DE
16 July 2024

57381855R00149